Caine Aaron

# Diary of a Failed Life Coach

# Contents

# Diary of a Failed Life Coach

Energy is life. Life is energy. Use it or be used.
  – Eddie King


Life is love. Don't play a cover.
  – Eddie King


Make your heart your blood brother.
  – Eddie King


I want to live. I want a life. Damn it; I want to feel.
  – Eddie King


Remember the light as it shines in your heart and connect with it. You are and always shall be Golden Love.
  – Eddie King


Cast into the light that which you desire and send into the world that which you are... And most of all, love.
  – Eddie King

When you separate yourself from yourself, bad things tend to happen.

    – Eddie King

# Introduction

Yesterday, I attended a life coaching convention to stay fresh in my coaching techniques. They suggest writing a journal. They say it's a good exercise for people to be completely uncensored. I'm going to write one for thirty days. Then I'll read it. If it works, I'll implement it to my patients.

Here's a little something about myself. My name is Eddie King. I'm not Asian even though my name sounds like it. I don't own a hotdog stand. I'm just a regular guy. I'm thirty-two and live a middle-class life in a middle-class town. Sometimes, I wish I moved to a big city like Los Angeles and became a movie star. That would be the life. Everyone would love me. Instead, I chose to help people. I've been a life coach for five years now. I have a few regular clients and some randoms that pop in for a boost. It's my alternative way of thinking that sets me apart from most people. Even the way I chose to become a life coach was a bit odd. I was on vacation at Venice Beach with my friend, Jon. It was just before sunset. We both have a good alcohol buzz and are strolling the boardwalk looking for action like people do when they're in high school. Zoltar the fortune teller machine catches my eye. It's a machine just like the one in the movie, "Big." I say to Jon,

– Maybe Zoltar can tell us what to do for the rest of the night.
– You pay, I'll play.

That's typical Jon. He never has any money. I say,

– I'm doing it. Give us some insight, Zoltar.

I put in a dollar, and Zoltar Speaks. He says some generic crap that is barely hearable due to the people walking past. Out pops a piece of paper the size of a parking garage ticket. On one side it says: "Zoltar Speaks." On the other is a fortune. I say,

– Jon, you ready for some answers?

– I'm ready for another drink or some tang before
my buzz wears off.

– The fortune reads: "You will bring sunshine
into someone's life."

Jon jokes,

– It says you're gonna be a life coach.

– Hmmm?

– Yo' coach, make my life better.

– Shut up. I'd be a good life coach.

– Yeah, you could coach yourself too.

– Fuck off. Let's drink at Sidewalk and
watch the sunset.

– Whatever you say, coach.

That was the start of that. The world gave me a sign, and I followed it. Everyone should look for signs.

Before the life coach convention, my life was pretty normal. I had a girl in the works. Her name is Nora, and she is glorious. Everything about her is top-notch. She's short with jet black hair. Her eyes are perfect blue. Gazing into them warms my whole body. When I think of her, one word comes to mind: goddess. Her body is near perfect. Her breasts are perfect C's. Her butt is a perfect crescent. Our bodies fit together perfectly. It's like I'm the peanut butter, and she's the jelly.

Our connection is undeniable. It's one that most people only dream of having. We're so blessed. It's love to the fullest degree. We don't say the words to each other, but we don't have to. The only catch is that she's married with kids and lives in another country.

Not sure what I expected to gain from this but our undeniable real-life connection needed to be acted upon. So, I did. We did. Nora makes me feel the best I ever felt. I get her glowing as well. Our relationship or rather our real-life moment lasted only two weeks.

Now she's gone back to her family, maybe gone forever. I hope not. Maybe she feels what I feel and will come back. I cry when I think of her. It's embarrassing when you cry in public particularly at a life coach convention. People believe that you're only there to help myself. They probably think I'm a quack. I assure you, I am not. Anyway, who cares what they think? It's my life. I choose it.

Currently, my life is going back to the way it was before Nora. I give all of my energy to help people get their lives on track, and there's never much left for me to feel anything of my own. It makes my life pretty bland. Maybe Nora will think of me when she's having sex with her husband. That makes me smile.

Nora thinks our connection is from a past life. It may be, but if we keep bumping into each other, it has to be destiny. We're undeniable. So meant to be. I'm going to cry now. I love you, Nora. Please come back. I want to feel something other than losing you.

# 1

## Day 1

I take my motorcycle to the shop to get a carb adjustment. The mechanic says it will cost $1000.00 because they have to clean the tank and fix something else as well. I say,

– That's a lot.

He smirks and says,

– That's the price.

– Is this cause you are the only shop in town, so you price gouge people?

– You can take your bike anywhere you want. The next town over perhaps. That's our price.

– I don't understand. It's just carbs.

– Well, understand because I ain't got time for this. You want us to fix them or not?

– A thousand dollars?

It's not in my nature to get negative but fuck them. A thought pops into my head. It's a memory of burning down my elementary school enemies' fort. They were older and always tried to run me over with their motorcycles. I can't help but think that if it happened once, then it could happen again.

The mechanic walks away. I say,

– Fine. What choice do I have? Bend over and...

– What did you say?

– I said do it.

– A $250 deposit by tomorrow or I'll put your bike on the street.

– Fine.

My defeated walk home is full of obsessing thoughts. Maybe I'll see the mechanic on the street late at night or in a grocery store parking lot. He doesn't know who he's messing with.

Laying in bed, I can't help but wonder where all of that negativity came from? That's not how to handle things. I'm better than that.

# 2

# Day 2

I coach a regular of mine. He's in his late thirties and can't get over his youth. He claims that money and possessions are the only things keeping him from happiness. My answer is the same every time:

– Happiness starts from within. Things can't fill the hole. Fill your hole with love. Happiness will follow. Embrace your love.

– What if rap music is right when they say everything is about money and bitches?

– You're basing your happiness on what rappers say?

– They have to be right because they all say the same thing.

I roll my eyes and say,

– It's just entertainment. It's not to be taken seriously.

– If only I had money, then everything would fall into place.

Sometimes it feels like I'm talking to a wall. I say,

– "Shine on you crazy diamond." God is in all of

us, and when we connect to that energy, you
have the ability to be all-time. So be all-time.
That's what rappers are doing.
- I'm not a rapper.
- Why not be a shining light of positivity and
abundance instead of worrying about things
you don't have? Maybe become a rapper.
- You're funny Doc.
- What's funny about it? Shine your light and
abundance will follow. So will everyone else.
- I'll work on it.

I pay the motorcycle shop the $250 deposit to start the work.
The manager is in a meeting with all of the mechanics. I drop
the money with the girl who works in parts. I know this because
the nameplate on her desk doesn't say her name. It reads "Parts
Department." She's a cute hipster looking girl with tattoos up
both her arms and jet black hair with bangs. She probably works
here to get a discount on her bike maintenance. She's cute.
After paying, I ask,
- How long have you worked here?
- This is my second day.
- Do you like it?
- It's okay. The manager is hot headed. He flips
out sometimes.
- Do you ride?
- I have a '76 Honda CB550.
- Nice.
The manager yells from the other room,
- Nancy, did you order the parts yet?
She replies,

4

– Not yet.
– How the hell are we supposed to fix bikes
without parts?
– I'm on it.
– Get the shit out of your brain and get to it.
That's what we pay you for.
– Yes, sir.
She smirks at me and gets on her computer. I say,
– You're the best thing about this shop. Have a
beautiful day.
– I'm over this shit. This is my last day.
– Then have a beautiful life. Always know that
you're the manifestation light and love.
Her eyes light up, and she smiles. This may be the first good
thing that happened to her all day. I'm glad I could help. She
says,
– Thank you. I needed that.
She answers the ringing phone. I exit.

A nice bottle of red table wine from France finishes out my
day. It's not the plan to finish the whole bottle, but I have no
one to help me drink it. Nora loves wine. Tears conclude the
night. I slur to anyone listening, which is no one.
– Why hasn't a lasting relationship happened for
me? It sucks being alone.

# 3

# Day 3

My life is pretty boring. My daily routine is the same every day. I wake up. Then brush my teeth. Think about doing push-ups and sit-ups. It rarely happens. Either I make coffee or get some at the coffee shop. I meet with people who need something from me. Then I ride my motorcycle the long way home through the park. On the exciting days, I park and hike around. Today isn't one of them. It's homeward bound. The TV comes on for background noise. "(500) Days of Summer" is on. I haven't seen it in a while so that it will fill my time nicely. The poor guy loses the love of his life. I can relate. I hope to find an Autumn someday.

A damn good chicken, broccoli, and almond butter panini is my dinner. Now that my belly is full, the night is for the taking. I probably won't take it anywhere. I sit in silence contemplating everything and nothing.

Writing in my journal seems like a good idea. The convention said journals are only useful if you allow yourself to be completely open. Here goes nothing: I'm happy to help people get back on track. Although, I'm not entirely sure I'm on track.

There are a lot of things I want to happen like a relationship. Not feel energy drained all of the time would be nice too.

My life coaching abilities consist of clients coming in and stealing my energy and using it to feel better. When these energy leeches use it all up, they come back for more. These leeches could be the cause of my boring life. They could be the cause of my lonely life. I want to live. I want a life. Damn it; I want to feel.

My long time friend, Jon calls me.
- Hey, Johnny boy.
- Get dressed.
- I am dressed.
- Not in your dippy coach clothes. Put on your get laid clothes. We are hitting the town. By town, I mean a party.
- My shit ain't dippy. Where at?
- The best bar in town...Friday's.
- Wow, are we going to share an app platter and see what us high rollers attract?
- Man, it's an office party. And not just any office party. The women in this office are hot. Not just hot either. We're talking Hollywood hot.
- What business?
- Who cares?
- What office?
- I forget. What's important is that we are going to bring sunshine into women's lives.
- You coaching me now?
- Get ready. I'm coming over.
- Don't. I want to stay in.

– Why because of Nora? You got to get out there,
man. That's the only way to get over her.

– Maybe.

– You're a bigger pussy that I thought.

– Fuck you, dude. We were real. That takes time.

– Pussy.

– Let me know how it goes. You there?

Jon hangs up on me. I grab the remote and search for a movie. "The Notebook" is on. That's more my speed.

# 4

## Day 4

My appointment book is empty today. A day to myself. When this happens, I usually have things to do like see Nora. Today, I don't have that liberty. Meditation will start my day. I'll see where that takes me.

  This journal writing thing is tedious. I'll stick it out. What kind of life coach would I be if I couldn't commit to change?

  I got a good cry in last night from watching "The Notebook." It felt like I was on my man period. None-the-less I feel refreshed like I got some stuff out. It's probably better that I didn't go out with Jon.

  Now some meditation for guidance is in order. I breathe and focus on my breath as it moves in and out of my body. As my connection grows toward my inner God, I practice moving energy around my body. I send it to my feet. I feel them tingle with delight. I move it to my elbows and pop it to my fingertips. My sole focus is on the energy moving about my body. Wherever I focus it to, it goes there and tingles me with delight. I'm working on a body swirl. Imagine a tornado swirling around in your body and then lifting you up. I'm not saying that I'm trying to fly. I'm trying to buzz and emit an explosion of light, not an explosion that will hurt people but rather help people.

This gets me thinking about superpowers. Do people have them? Are people miserable because they don't connect and use them? This question is one of the things that got me into coaching in the first place.

My superpower is the ability to move energy through my body and pass it to other people. My power gives people the light and ability to feel good. It gives me the satisfaction that I've helped someone but drains me at the same time. The bitter part is that people can take it from me. When this happens, I'll fall into a massive depression. Sometimes even suicidal thoughts will plague me in my down period.

The other thing is that my superpower attracts energy leeches. A lot of mediums come into my world. It can't be certain what they want. Maybe it's the fact that we both have harnessed our power. Or it could be that they see my energy and want to steal it.

I eat a turkey sandwich for lunch then meditate the rest of the day.

# 5

# Day 5

I'm coaching a thirty-something fellow who doesn't follow through on things. If only it were as easy as telling this guy to man-up. Adults follow through on things. That's what they do. His problems stem from the fact that he has ideas about how his life should be and what he wants to happen. But he never does anything to get to that point, so they just stay ideas. I say,

    - Your ideas are your inner voice. That light is
    trying to shine through, but you won't let it.
    Your fear likes being in control because it keeps
    you safe. Doing nothing is better than failing.
    Do you agree?
    - I guess so. But, that's like not voting. I vote.
    - Do you have ideas about stuff but end up going
    along with friends?
    - I do, but that's just life happening.
    - Or when you do take control of a situation, do
    you listen to the advice of others?
    - That is my time to shine not theirs.
    - Do you think that could be fear running your

life?

– No.

– Do you feel you second-guess yourself to the
point that you never do anything that you want
to do?

– I'm not a scaredy-cat. You better watch your
tongue. I'm done with your shit.

He tries to cut the session short. I grab his arm and say,

– Wait.

With a flash, my energy storms through my body and into
him.

– Please, good sir, feel the power that is within
you. Allow your light to shine. When you are in
doubt, remember that you are the manifestation
of light. You are the manifestation of love.

Listen to your heart, and it will guide you.

He looks at me with a disheartening stare. He's not buying it.
I continue,

– Swear to me right here and now that you will
always follow your heart.

He looks at me then looks away. Seemingly reluctant, he says,

– I swear that I will listen to my heart.

His words make me smile. I say,

– Pinky swear?

He looks at me and says,

– Too much.

He gets up. I hold my hand up for a high-five and say,

– Make your heart your blood brother and listen
to it.

– My heart is my blood brother, and I will listen
to it.

We high-five.

Today, I earn a hike in the woods. It seems appropriate to keep this good feeling going.

The air is fresh out here in the woods. It smells of life. It reminds me that without these plants, the earth wouldn't be alive. It reminds me that everything is connected. A deep breath and some positivity fill me. With my eyes closed, I hope to connect with the energy of the world. I flash back to when I lived on a farm. Those were some happy times. It flashes me back to when I used to live in the Chamber Hills Apartments and running from those damn motorcycles. Having to dive into jagger bushes to keep from getting run over. Those days weren't fun. The bike shop hasn't called me back yet. That is something I should check on.

The woods are peaceful. Just being here calms me. I find a rock that isn't covered with moss and sit. I clear my head with some deep breaths. It feels good to connect with Mother Earth. A calmness fills me with delight.

I hear voices coming toward me. It sounds like a girl, and two guys are joking around. I want to get up and move but don't. I listen.

– Baby, come this way. Sit on Daddy's lap.

– He's not your Daddy, I am.

– Neither of you are. Now, where is this thing you want to show me? ...Get your fucking hands off me!

– Isn't this what you wanted?

– Fuck you!

– What did you think was going to happen? Two

guys and a girl in the middle of the woods.

– Why don't you show us your tits!?

– Why don't you go fuck yourself!? This isn't
funny.

– Where do you think you're going?

The sound of a smack and a body hitting the ground echoes through the woods. My eyes open abruptly. They aren't joking. My phone doesn't work here so I can't call the cops. They would probably say don't get involved because I might get hurt.

What about her? It sounds like they're ripping her clothes off. One of their hands muffles her screams. I can't just sit here. I hear one of them say,

– I will cut you like the pig you are. Scream
again. I dare you.

If I can get a view of their faces, then I can be a witness. I sneak down to get a better view. It's hard to do because of all of the brush on the ground. Every step has to be gentle and slow. I'll be dead if they see me. They'll come after me. No witnesses. I've seen movies. One of them says,

– It's my turn. Fuck man! Come on, come on!

– Dude, it'll take longer if you don't shut up.
Suck her tits or something.

I'm able to make my way to a view. She's crying. One kid is fucking her from behind at a fast rate. The other is stroking his dick. I'm still too far away to see their faces.

My body freezes from disbelief. Rape shouldn't be in my world. The first thing I think to do is throw a rock to the other side of the woods. When it hits the ground, maybe they'll think someone is over there. I do it. One of them yells,

– Take one step closer, and I'll shoot.

The one fucking her stops. He pulls a handgun from his jean

jacket that is sitting on the ground. The other guy wastes no time. He mounts the girl the same way his friend had and says,
    – What the fuck is that?
    – Insurance.
He pushes the gun to her head and says,
    – Die, die my darling.
I practically shit myself and fall backward.

I wake up cold and damp on the ground. No one is around. I slowly get up and check the area. It's almost dark and very hard to see. My cellphone flashlight guides me to the location of the rape. I fall twice. There's no sign of abuse. There's no blood, no clothes, no anything.
    – Fuck. Was that real?
The bump on my head is real. There's some blood around it, and it hurts when I touch it. Why is there no evidence other than my painful head? I'll come back tomorrow.
Making my way out of the forest is one of the more frightening things I've ever done. The dark sounds of the woods are everywhere. Every sound could be them running up on me. My body tenses but I can't just stand here. It's too dark to run even with the phone light, but I do anyway. When I get out of the forest, my car is still in the same place.
    – Thank God.
The drive home is equally as scary. Every time a car drives up behind me, I can't help but think it's them following me. It takes a half hour to do a ten-minute drive.
    I tend to my wound while drinking myself to sleep.
    – Did that actually happen? Why is there no
evidence? I have to go back in the morning.
Should I call the cops? Surely, she has already.

# 6

# Day 6

Before I say anything, I want to say that my ex-girlfriend, Nora, contacted me today. She's the one who moved to Canada. The one who I'm head-over-heels in love with still. Did she contact me just to fuck with me because she knows it will make me sad to think that we can't be together? Or did she contact me because she too knows that we're supposed to be together?

Every time I think of Nora my world only revolves around her. My entire day is spent hoping that we can be together and when we can't, I get as sad as a clown and cry. Her text reads: "Are you okay? ;)." She is so selfish sometimes.

When I sat down to write in this thing, I wanted to talk about the rape, but instead, all I can think about is Nora. Her bright blue eyes give me a warm fuzzy feeling inside. She's the only person I will freely give all of my energy. That scares me. It also scares me that we can't be together unless she says so. I love you, Nora.

Back to the rape. When I wake this morning, my whole body felt eerie. It feels like death is somewhere around me.

I flick through the TV channels in search of proof that the rape happened. My other hand feels for the lump on my head. It's there and still sore.

There is nothing about rape on the news. My headache says otherwise. I could have fallen and smacked my head while meditating and everything was a dream. That's an option. It seems more likely that I slipped while trying to help her.

- Why is there nothing on the news?

Maybe she didn't report it yet. One would think if something like that happened, the first thing you would do is go to the police.

I go about my day. I think about doing push-ups and sit-ups, then shower, enjoy my morning coffee, and center myself for the day with meditation.

The phone rings. It's the motorcycle shop.

- Is this Eddie King?

- Yes, sir.

- We had a slight problem.

- Oh?

- While flushing the tank of rust, it got knocked over and dented.

- What? How bad?

- It's better if you come and see it. We're looking for a replacement but can't find one in the same color.

I say,

- My bike is completely original. I brought it in that way, and I want to pick it up that way.

- We are sorry, sir. We'll keep looking, but it's not looking good.

- So what you're telling me is that my original
bike will no longer be original, and it's your
fault. What kind of shit is that?
- Sir, you could have taken it somewhere else,
and we appreciate your business but these
things happen, and we apologize.
- That's supposed to make it okay? I'm coming
down there. We'll settle this like men.

I slam down the phone hard enough that the phone or the
table should have broke. Neither did.

The only thing going through my head while driving to the
shop is how this is going to play out.

1. They found a tank.

2. It's not as bad as they say and I can live with it as long as
my repair is free, which will save me a thousand dollars.

3. It is bad, and the bike will never be the same again.

If number three is the option, what will I do? Kick over all the
bikes in the lot. Maybe throw paint bombs in their yard on all of
the bikes causing them a massive bill. I could always be positive
that they will find a very similar tank and treat me accordingly.
I could always burn the place down.

As I'm pulling up to the shop, I hear on the radio that a girl has
committed suicide by jumping off of an eight-story building.
My foot slams the car to a stop. That could be her. Maybe
she couldn't live with herself and ended her life. What if they
killed her and made it look like a suicide? There are three main
hospitals in the area. My motorcycle can wait.

The first hospital I check is the county hospital. They said
no DOA's have arrived in the last 24 hours. They ask why I'm
asking. I say no reason and exit immediately.

The second hospital tells me to hang on. I wait while the receptionist calls it in. My hearing is good. I listen. She says,
– We have a suspicious character asking about
dead bodies that just arrived.
I high-tail it to my car and speed out of there.

The third hospital wants me to wait in a hospital room. I check the door to look around, and I'm locked in. My senses pick up death in the air. It's the same feeling that I woke with. Panic runs through me. Is it panic that I found her or panic that I'm trapped?
I brought a knife just in case. I use it to jimmy open the window. The room is on the second floor. Twelve feet down sure does look high. I hear the doorknob of my room wiggle. Scared as hell, I jump. Upon hitting the ground, I roll. It's how I learned it in my youth. I dust myself off and run. Voices from the window scream,
– Get back here!
– Someone stop him!
One guy in a nurse's uniform chases me. He stops midway through the parking lot. I run into the woods. I'll go back for my car when things cool down.

I have to cancel on Eva, a client because I can't get to my car. I suggest that she stay positive and only focus on the love in her life and that her mantra for the day be: "I am the manifestation of light. I am the manifestation of love." If she repeats this whenever she is down, she should be able to change her vibration to positive.

My last stop before going home is the woods where the rape

took place. It's on the verge of getting dark, so I'll have to be quick. There seems to be no evidence of anything, not even a broken branch. If only she had dropped something. The only blood I find is where I smacked my head. The rape pops into my head.

– Tell me you fucking love it. Say it. Say it bitch!
– It's my turn boner. Hurry up.
– Die, die my darling.

Searching for the dead girl takes up my whole day. I'll meditate on it. Hopefully, the answer is that this isn't the same girl and I am just paranoid.

I love you, Nora.

# 7

## Day 7

You know what? Fuck this shit. I don't need this crap in my life. None of this should be happening to me. I'm taking off work today. No TV or computer either. I have one appointment and cancel it due to a family emergency. You know what the family emergency is? It's the fact that I need a break. I don't need to try so incredibly hard to make everyone else feel better when I can't currently make myself feel better. Well, guess what? I do make myself feel better. I don't answer the phone. I DON'T DO ANYTHING EXCEPT TELL THE WORLD TO FUCK OFF. Today is my day. I may not accomplish anything today. But my relationship with this gin bottle is better than ever.

　– World, when I'm back, you better be ready.
　None of this crap. It's me versus you. And I'm
　coming like a whirlwind. I am the manifestation
　of light. I am the manifestation of love.
　Fuck everything!

And, I love you all.

I got two shots of gin left. One for me and me.

…Peace.

# 8

## Day 8

What happened yesterday was something that needed to happen. Not necessarily the drinking all day but the recharge. Flaking on a client is never good. Even if I did meet with her, I wouldn't have had anything to give? My energy was low.

The first thing I do upon getting to work is to check my messages and get the mail. Eva, who I canceled on, left a message:
  – "Eddie, I needed you yesterday. Things aren't
  going the way you said they would. I've tried
  over and over to Stay Golden, and the only thing
  going through my head is that doing that is
  living in denial. Just because I don't focus on it
  doesn't mean it doesn't exist. Denying my
  feelings makes me feel even worse. I would
  like to meet today if I'm still around."

As fast as lightning, I call her. She doesn't answer. Speeding down the street, I have one thing in mind, "this can't be happening." I roll through every stop sign as a Californian would. Her house is just ahead. Sweat begins to roll down my forehead. The car door stays open as I run to her. I knock. No answer. The door is locked. The back door is also locked. I look in the windows. No luck. Then I see her. She has a towel wrapped around her head. She's naked otherwise.

– Oh, thank God.

She sees me. I wave at her and smile. She screams and quickly covers herself. It's too late. I saw everything. I wish I had a girl that looks like that. She storms off. She comes out of the house with a handgun pointed at me.

– You fucking fuck. Get off of my property
before I blow your Goddamn head off. I'm
calling the police!

– Eva. It's me Eddie, your life coach.

– Is this what you do, spy on your patients? You
pervert.

– The message you left sounded like you were
going to kill yourself. I wanted to stop you.
That's why I'm here.

Eva Dials three numbers on her phone.

– Hello, yes, I would like to report a peeping
Tom. Can you send someone? I have a gun
pointed at him, so he isn't going anywhere.
What was I supposed to do? Please hurry.

She hangs up. The look in her eye changes. She appears to have emotions, which is something we've been working to bring out. She usually is all surface. She says,

– You care about me?

– Of course, I care about you. For one, you're a
great person. For two, you have some of the
deepest-rooted beauty I have ever come across.

24

Your light shines bright even though you don't
let it. But I see it. I see who you really are.
- So you know about me?
- Yes.
She puts the gun to her head.
- Wait. I don't know anything about you. Don't
do this.
- I can't live with myself.
- Whatever happened, we can fix it. Focus on
your inner light. Let that guide you.
- I don't have any light left.
Sirens approach. Uncertainty fills me. The only thing I can
think to say is,
- I love you, Eva.
Her eyes fix on me. I continue,
- I love everything about you. Ever since we
met, I can't help these feelings. It's as if the
thought of you consumes me. It's like
everything I do; I do it for you.
- You're just saying that.
- I'm not. This has never happened to me before.
I don't know if I can go on without you. It's like
there is something pulling us together. Don't
you feel it?
- You're my life coach.
- Well, think about it. The cops are coming, and I
don't want to go to jail. And I don't want you to
die. Please put down the gun, Eva.
It looks as if she is considering it. Her eyes now look at me
differently, but we're running out of time. It sounds like the
cops are right out front. I'm fucked, but she's alive. Eva lowers

the gun and says,

    – Hide in the pantry. I'll handle this.

Without saying a word, I do. The cops get there just as Eva slams the door shut. The only thing going through my head is, "why did I say that?" I don't feel that way. Yeah, Eva has a beautiful body, but she is my patient. I can't help but think this is all Nora's fault. On the bright side, Eva isn't dead. Yeah but, what happens when she finds out that I just said that to save her? She's not even my type. I like short girls with black hair. She's a tall blonde. The pantry door swings open. For an instant, I think this is the end. She smiles at me. I smile back in relief. She pulls herself into the pantry and closes the door. She kisses me like a lost lover would. I want to resist. I do at first. Then it feels good to be wanted. My embrace becomes hers. In my head she becomes Nora. I've been waiting for this moment. We have sex in her pantry, then her kitchen, and then her bed.

# 9

## Day 9

The sound of someone banging on the front door wakes me. I put my robe on and check it out. The hardwood floor is unusually cold today. Each step makes me think of being trapped in a house on a winter day. The sun shining through the window is bright and makes it hard to see. The knocking seems to be getting louder. It becomes my beacon. The sun blasts me in the face as I open the door. It makes it practically impossible to see. If the two people standing there wanted to kill me, it would be quite easy for them. My eyes adjust, and the silhouettes become two uniformed cops. One of them has a mean look on his face which is weird because I haven't done anything.

– Can I help you, officers?

– Are you Eddie King?

– Yes, sir. Isn't it a little early for house calls?

– Is anyone here with you?

– It's just me.

– We're going to need you to come with us.

I want to run, and I didn't even do anything.

– Excuse me?

– Let's not make this difficult.

- Can I at least put some clothes on?
- No.

They cuff and place me in the back of their car. I inquire about what this is about, but they won't tell me anything except to shut up. When we get to the station, I get searched. It doesn't take long because I'm only wearing a bathrobe. Next, I get fingerprinted.

They give me some slippers and put me in a holding cell with four other people. One of them is a three-hundred-pound biker looking guy with a goatee. He is sleeping. Another one is a gangbanger looking kid. He's black and is wearing saggy jeans. He's pacing back and forth. He has to hold his jeans up with his hand. The other two look to be about twenty. They seem to be acting hard, so no one messes with them. I sit on the empty spot beside the biker. Keeping my mouth shut seems like the best plan. One of the young kids says,

- What are you a streaker?
- Are you talking to me?
- I don't see anyone else wearing a robe.
- I don't know.
- You don't know if you're a streaker?
- I don't know why I'm in here. I didn't do anything.

The gangbanger never breaks stride and chimes in,

- None of us did anything. This is racial profiling.

The biker's body leans over my way, and his head rests on mine. I've now become a human pillow which sucks. The same young kid continues,

- Well, you look like a streaker.
- I ain't no fucking streaker. I'm a life coach.

– Then you better coach yourself, you boner.

He and his friend laugh. They high-five each other. The gangbanger bends over from his laugh, and his pink boxer shorts are on full display. The biker begins to snore. I say,

– Why are you in here?

– Apparently, mailbox baseball is frowned upon
in this town. And having a few dozen eggs in
the car doesn't help much neither.

His buddy shoves him to shut up then gets in my face and says,

– Who asked you old man? Mind your own
fucking business.

– I didn't mean anything by it. If I were to say
something, it would be that you're vibrating
negatively. We can work on that. I can help you
get that back to positive. You got to Stay
Golden and good things will come your way.

– Like yourself? Fuck you old man.

His friend joins him in front of me. Now they're both mad dogging me. My mouth dries. A pit in my stomach opens. They continue in unison,

– Die, die my darling.

If I could kiss my ass goodbye, this is probably a good time to do it. The biker rolls over and cuddles me like I'm his teddy bear. His massive arm is around me which deters the kids for a moment. One of them steps on my foot. I want to jump up but don't want to wake the biker. Instead, the pain comes out through my eyes. The kid tries to step on my foot again. We're almost tap dancing. I dodge as he stomps. The gangbanger starts beat-boxing and rapping,

– "It sucks being on a boat with Uncle Cracker,

'Cause he shows up always bringing disaster.
One day his ship will sink like the Titanic,
And my rap will become gigantic,
Until he puts me behind bars to feel safe,
If only all crackers would go to Mars,
Then everything would be great."

His rapping distracts me for a second. One of the kid stomps on my foot as hard as he can. I scream,

– You mother fucker! I will fucking gut you like
the pig you are.

I try my hardest to get up, but the biker's arm tightens around my body.

– Get your fucking arm off of me. I'll kill your
fat ass too!

The young kid who didn't step on my foot says,

– Wow, dude, you got some serious issues. No
wonder you're in here.

– Fuck you. You entitled douche bag. I'll gut you
too!

The biker begins squeezing me hard. I can feel the air leaving my body. I start gasping for air. The biker says,

– Cool it. If you don't, I will.

Light-headedness overtakes me. The only thing I can do is tap out on his arm and pray. Just as my vision is about to tunnel to all black, I hear a voice say,

– Eddie King.

The arm restricting my breathing softens. My vision comes back. Deep breaths bring me back to reality. The guard opens the door of the cell. He says,

– Everything okay in here?

Everyone responds,

- Yes, sir.

It's hard to breathe. The biker pushes me to my feet. That is probably the only way I would have gotten there.  The gangbanger stops me from falling over. The cop notices,

- Made some friends, did you?

The two young kids say,

- Happy to meet you, sir. Remember to Stay
Golden and good things will happen.

I look back at him and say,

- That's my line.

The young kid motions to me that he's going to slice my throat. The cop leads me away. He takes me into an interrogation room and sits me in a chair. He leaves. It's the longest five minutes in history.

Two plain-clothed cops enter.  One of them sits while the other one leans against the wall. They study me. My eyes dart around waiting for one of them to say something. I break the silence and say,

- What is this about?

- You tell us.

- Don't know. You arrested me. Never read me my rights. Then put me in a cell with some infuriated kids. And you want me to tell you?

- You're not under arrest. We detained you for questioning.

- For what? I didn't do anything.

- Does the name Eva Sanders mean anything to you?

- She says you like peeping around her house.

- That. I'm a life coach, and she's one of my

patients. I had an emergency two days ago and had to cancel our appointment. She sounded suicidal, so I rushed over to her house to see if she was okay. I was looking in the windows but only to see if she was okay.

– So you admit that you're a peeping Tom.

– With good intentions. I spoke with her after, and she seemed to understand. She definitely thanked me for my help. Can you call her or something?

The cop leaning against the wall says,

– A peeping Tom life coach? It sounds like you're not very good at your job.

The other cop says,

– Coaching people to be perverts everywhere.

– Honest, I'm not a pervert. I just wanted to help her. I got too drunk to work the day before and was feeling guilty, so I rushed over.

– An alcoholic, peeping Tom, life coach. You're a real piece of work. I think we should lock him up and throw away the key.

– Please. I swear on my grandmother's grave that I didn't mean it like that. I honestly just want to help people. I may not be perfect, but my teachings help people.

If ever there was a time that I needed a superpower, it's now. As indiscreet as possible, I focus my energy hoping to create a burst of positivity to get the officers to change their minds. There is usually a sequence of movements I have to go through. Instead, I close my eyes and palms. With a focused burst, I simultaneously open my hands and my eyes forcing out all of the positive energy I can muster. The cop standing up laughs and says,

– What was that? Were you farting or something?

This guy is a joke.

The cop sitting down says,

– If we catch you peeping again, your ass is going to jail.

– They would like a handsome guy like yourself.

– Thank you so much. I wasn't peeping and will never do so. You have my word.

The cop sitting slams his fist on the table and says,

– I don't ever want to see you again. You're free to go.

Both the cops walk out. I sit there a moment then run out.

# 10

# Day 10

Friends are hard to come by so usually I just hang out by myself. When I'm not doing that, occasionally I hang with Jon. He and I have been friends since high school. He works as a bartender at Vitiello's Italian Restaurant. He always gets free alcohol from there. He may steal it. I'm not sure. It does the job either way. My first phone call after getting out of jail is to invite him over. Hopefully, he can help me figure this whole thing out.

Jon lightly knocks then walks in. I'm not sure why he knocks at all. No one can hear it. The sound of the door closing is my cue. I pour two tequila shots and greet him in the hallway. Starting with shots is our ritual. The first words out of my mouth are,

– You won't believe the week I'm having. Cheers.

I hand him the smaller shot. He says,

– Cheers. To things looking up.

– And to sharing our Golden Love with everyone
we meet.

After slamming the shots, he turns sports on the TV. I'm not that big into sports, but he is. I pour us two more shots then tell him of my week. Everything comes out, the rape I may have witnessed, the girl who committed suicide, going to jail, and

lastly my motorcycle tank. After telling him all of this, he walks
away. He brings us back shots and says,
   – That sucks, but my news may be worse.
   – That seems hard to believe considering.
   – I'm moving back to Ohio.
   – Why would anyone do that?
   – My mom got real sick, and there's no one to
take care of her.
   – But what about your life? What about all of
the things you want to do?
   – She raised me. I owe her.
   – She raised you to fly. So fly.
   – This is how life works. It's a cycle.
   – But...
   – There are no buts. This is life happening.
   – So you're just going to drop everything that
you worked your whole life for to take care of
your mom? Couldn't you hire someone?
   – That's how it works, man. You give back.
   – I give every day. I give energy. I give life
coaching.
   – That's your job. I'm talking real giving, to the
people that matter, to your family and friends.
Really to anyone who needs it.
   – I guess.
I find some composure and continue,
   – As this new chapter begins, don't lose
sight of who you are. Your job doesn't define
you.
   – Thanks, coach.
   – See, I told you I'd be a good life coach.

- You're not so bad, I suppose.
- I'm going to miss you, Jon.
- Now you got no excuse not to get a girlfriend.

This time I leave the room. I come back with the bottle. I pour us shots and say,

- This is the worst week ever.

# 11

## Day 11

Nora contacted me. It sounds like she is having second thoughts about where she stands with us. For her to show this is a dream come true for me. But I'm not sure it's a good thing. I've been trying so hard to get over her, and now she validates our magical experience. If only there were a road map to map out how to deal with these things. It took some thinking and here is the email that I'm going to send her:

Life Coach Eddie would say to trust your inner light. Let it guide you. It will not steer you wrong. It is the true you that which is stripped of all things programmed. When you connect with your light, then you connect with God. There is where all answers lie.

Sometimes connections happen. We don't always know why. Some say past lives. What we do know is that it is special when they do. And these moments of connection should be strived for because these are the moments that remind us that we are alive. People come into each other's lives for a reason. This is certain. Sometimes it is for selfish reasons, other times for the benefit of the other (Thank you), and sometimes for mutual benefit. Either way, when it happens, it is special and should be acted upon. Sometimes that is the extent of it. Sometimes it is the collision that was necessary to propel us forward. Other times it may be more. Only when we connect with our inner God will all of the answers be apparent to us.

The fact that we have these moments is the biggest blessing of all. Take from them what you will because connections happen for a reason.

Remember the light as it shines in your heart and connect with it. You are and always shall be Golden Love. Stay Golden Ponygirl.

P.S. This will be my last email because again, your response is the only thing I'm looking forward to every day. These thoughts consume me. It's hard for me to do anything else. All I want to do is... I'm not used to dealing with this kind of emotion. I too have to listen to my inner light. For now, it has told me to listen to a song titled: "You Can't always Get What You Want" by The Rolling Stones.

Love Love Forever
Eddie

P.P.S Cue my tears here.

# 12

## Day 12

The coffee shop is where my day starts.  It's marginally full. There are four people in line in front of me and half of the tables have people.  A black girl is standing in front of me.  She has super shiny straight black hair.  That is something you don't see often. I'm talking about her fancy hair. Maybe I should tap her on the shoulder and tell her so. What if she is ugly? I feel so juvenile right now.

There is a newspaper sitting on a table. I'll read that instead. The same shit different day is the subtext as usual for the paper. That is until I get to page two. The headline reads: "Life Coach Fails!  Coaches his client to suicide." I have to look around because I can't believe my eyes.  The article says that Eddie King, Mary Levitt's life coach told her to see only the positive. How did they know it was me? It says that this denial is what kept her from seeing the true colors of people and got her in trouble. It says that in her suicide note, she said it was her life coaches fault that she is at this point. They say it's all my fault. I wrinkle up the paper and throw it on the ground.

    – Damn you!

The black girl in front of me turns. She's twenty-something

with big brown eyes and lips. She has the kind of lips you want to kiss you. Her face is shiny and done up like her hair. With a reprimanding tone, she says,

– You shouldn't talk like that.

– Don't worry. That wasn't toward you. I'm a life coach.

– Then you should know not to say that. Ever.

With a smirk, I say,

– I'm having a rough day.

– So coach yourself. Don't take that shit out on me.

As she turns around to order, her hair hits me in the eyes. It feels like needles pricking them. I want to scream, but instead, I Stay Golden and say,

– I said damn you because I am in the paper today. I'm sorry.

– Are you the failed life coach?

– Damn it. You don't even know the details.

– Hey, everyone, this is the failed life coach they were talking about in the paper.

Everyone stops and looks me. It feels like I'm the new kid who farted during a placement test in elementary school. The black girl gives me an evil smirk as she walks off. I watch her go. She's kind of pretty for a bitch.

Everyone is looking at me and snickering. Panic sets in. The barista asks for my order. I say,

– Large coffee with no room.

The barista evilly smirks as she takes my money. It looks like she is telling the other person behind the counter who I am. They are snickering and glancing at me. She gives me my coffee, and I say,

- What's so funny?
- Nothing. Have a good day.

I don't drop my change in her tip jar like I usually do. The crinkled up paper that I threw on the ground comes with me as I exit.

I drive. Anywhere away from here would be better than here. The best place would be the woods or home. I'll drink if I go home. I call Jon,

- Word up, Homie.
- Dude, I'm driving right now.
- Me too, how are things?
- How do you think? My butt hurts. This truck is uncomfortable. I'm full of uncertainty.
Everything is peachy.
- The newspaper fucked me.
- What does that mean?
- There was an article saying that a failed life coach is the reason a girl committed suicide. I was her life coach.
- There goes business.
- I'm royally fucked.
- You could always move to Cleveland.
- I think it was the girl who was raped.
- It's possible, but that was never reported.
- This is my new life goal. I will make this right and clear my name.
- You'll probably have a lot of time on your hands but don't.
- I got to go.
- Stay out of it!

I hang up and pull into the liquor store. If I don't get something to calm me down, I'm going to freak the fuck out. How could Mary blame me? It's not living in denial. It's choosing to focus on what you want.

A car parks beside me. Two shiny-faced boys jump out. One of them is wearing a cape. They run around their car and mine playing tag. Their mom yells for them to stop. The little kid with the cape stops in front of my car. Our eyes meet like we are in a stand-off. He smiles and waves. I smirk and nod. He runs into the store with his mom. A thought pops into my head. Would all of this be happening if I were a family man? Or would I just be dealing with my wife and kids? Is this the kind of stuff Nora deals with? Oh, sweet Nora. I drive off without buying anything.

I park in my regular parking spot outside the woods. I run into the woods. I pass the place of the alleged rape. It was never reported. Maybe it never happened. Should I leave it alone like Jon said?

I stop to catch my breath. The rape flashes in my head. Her screams echo in my head. The two guys holding their dicks over top of her. The gun. If only I could have seen their faces. I run hoping to shake the images. I run hoping to shake everything.

A spot where the sun breaks through the trees is where I end up. It's deep into the woods. I've never been in this far. It's silent here except for the rustling of the bushes when the wind blows. Shade covers me for a moment bringing a chill with it. The smell here reminds me of my youth. It reminds me of running from the motorcycles as they tried to kill me. I put my arms out and look to the sky. I say,

– Woods, if you can hear me, take the negative

from me and eat it up so only the good remains.
I know you're alive. I know you can hear me.
Cleanse me of this pain. Help me see the new
world. Help me live. Help me feel good.

# 13

## Day 13

Every Monday between 215 p.m. and 3 p.m. open yourself up and give the world your gifts. Open yourself to receive. Give the love. Feel the love. Feel the energy as it flows through you. Feel it as it vibrates your hands and tingles your toes. Feel one with it as it races through your body like fire. Feel the connection with this light and accept it's energy. Cast into the light that which you desire and send into the world that which you are. And most of all, love. (especially you Nora)

I wish I had someone to love and to love me back.

I check my life coach voicemail. My mailbox is full. Every message is the same. It is some organization wanting to ask me some questions about the suicide. I don't know anything about it. Nor do I want to talk about it. Once people see my face, then my business will be over no matter where I go. The final message is from Officer Dave. He wants me to come down to the station.

The urge to drink comes upon me as I park. My last time in

the police station wasn't fun. Those two young kids were such assholes the way they teamed up on me. The gangbanger rapper was funny rapping about Uncle Cracker. I wonder if he knows that's a band.

Inside the police station, they direct me to an interrogation room. Thankfully, it's not the same room, or my defenses would be sky-high. Officer Dave enters. He's a tall, slender gentleman. He looks to be in his early fifties. His aura is imposing. He sits and says,

– How's it feel to be a local celebrity?

– Not as good as I thought.

– I can imagine. It looks like you were just here.

– That was a misunderstanding. That's all.

– You seem to be involved in some things. Is this something we should worry about?

– I thought you invited me here to talk, not to interrogate.

With a wink, he says,

– You'd know if I were interrogating you. You wouldn't like it.

– So what is it that you wanted to talk about?

– What can you tell me about Mary Levitt? What was she like?

– She was normal with typical problems. You know like, uncertain of her life direction and wasn't sure why she was alone. The usual stuff.

– Can you tell me what she was really like?

– Patient-Doctor privilege.

– You're not a doctor. So spill it, or I'll lock you up for withholding evidence.

– Like a lot of people, she was caught up in a

negative trap. She couldn't/wouldn't understand that she was the source of all of her problems. A few bad things happened to her, and she shuts down. She closed herself off from the light that shines in everyone. She was only allowing the negative stuff of the world to affect her.

– The world is negative?

– You don't think so?

– Go on.

– It's not entirely negative, but it is easy to get caught up in stuff. This is what happened to her. She got caught up in lack. She was never content. She always wanted more. She couldn't fathom why people weren't open to her. She was pretty, and no one gave her the time of day. That was what she always said. Eventually, when you go down the negative road, it will take you to the bottom unless you become aware of it and actively change it. That is what I was trying to help her do.

– Closed off her inner light, fell into a negative trap, you sound like a life coach.

– Thank you. If you ever need anything, feel free to call.

– I'll pass.

– Did she have any friends that she would talk about?

– Not really. She seemed always to be alone. Why are you asking? She committed suicide.

– It just seems weird to me that a beautiful girl like that would kill herself.

- I don't know. I thought she was on the up-
swing.
- Is there anything else you can think of that
could help?
The rape flashes in my head. Jon said not to get involved. He's probably right. I have enough problems right now. I say,
- No, sir.
- If you do, can you call me?
He hands me his card and then his hand to shake. I'm scared to shake his hand because my palms are sweaty. Hopefully, he won't think something is up. He gives my hand a good squeeze and looks me in the eyes,
- Thanks for coming in.
- Anything to help.

I would love to go on a date to make me forget all of this crap.

It's 230 a.m. It feels like I haven't slept a wink. One question is keeping me awake. Why didn't I tell Officer Dave about the rape?

I look around, and there's nothing but snow and trees. I am speeding by the trees like they're standing still. Ahead of me is a berm and a jump. I'm wearing a Pittsburgh Steelers jacket and yellow gloves. I'm eight years old. My hands grip the boomerang steering wheel of my runner sled for dear life. My eyes begin to water from the 20-degree weather but most of all from the sheer speed. The jump is just ahead. My eyes close as I catch air. My eyes open and my hand rises in the victory of awesomeness. Upon landing, the sled hits a few banks then ends up in the street. I use my head to stop me from landing in the street

47

by slamming it into the snow fence that borders our property. When I get up, red is the only color around me. There's red in the snow. There's red on my jacket. There's red in my eyes. As I walk back to the house, a path of blood follows me. I don't feel anything but amusement for all the blood.

I open my eyes. I'm still in bed. My fingers run across the indented scar that has been on the hairline of my forehead for so long. I feel the new bump on the back of my head. It's just a slight bump and a scab now. It doesn't hurt anymore. I roll over and go to sleep.

# 14

## Day 14

I make coffee at home. I check my voicemail. Sure as shit, not even one. What irks me is that Jon didn't check back on me. Out of sight out of mind, I guess. Today would be a good day to do push-ups and sit-ups. That passes as just a mere thought like usual.

It seems best to lay low today. Practicing energy throwing will be my focus. You can't hone your skills if you don't practice. My energy is now at the point that I can throw it through my body into my hands anytime I want. It feels like handfuls of fire. It burns with delight. My hands seem to be the outlet. It's not like I have to do a superhero pose to throw it, but sometimes I do. My directional skills need a bit of work. I've been trying to move an inanimate object. That isn't my superpower. My superpower is telepathy through energy transference. Just today I thought about maggots, and there they were crawling out of my trash can. Luckily, I heard the call and got them out before they overtook my kitchen floor. I can also touch people with energy. Obviously, it's what makes me a good life coach. I've been working on long distance passing. I'm going to do a test. I'm going to attempt to send a long distance message.

# 15

## Day 15

No one has gotten back to me yet. I shouldn't say no one. I should say, Nora. I'm horrible. I just don't want to shake the feeling of love that flows inside of me when I think of her. My level of feeling has already dissipated some. My heart is trying so hard to hold on to it for dear life.

My cellphone buzzes. Hopefully, it's a client. I'm going to need some income to pay my bills. If it's not a client, please be Nora. It's neither. It's Tammy. She's one of my ex-girlfriends. This is unexpected. Her text reads: "Hey stranger, it's been a while. I was thinking of you yesterday. Figured I'd give you a call. Want to get coffee and catch up? I'm free right now."

We meet at the coffee shop. It's crowded as usual. I find a table outside. My large coffee with no room keeps me occupied while I wait.

Nervousness begins to fill my body. My defenses go up. Fingers tap on my shoulder. I turn. It's Tammy. She looks more put together than when we went out. She is wearing hip-hugging dark blue hipster jeans and a jean jacket. She has a Ramones' T-shirt underneath. There's a slight aura of light around her. I give her a hug.

- Hey, Tammy, you look good. Love the shirt.
- Thanks, you too.
- Stop. I know you're just saying that.

She says,

- You have a glow about you, Eddie. It's something I haven't seen before.
- Oh, stop. Do you want a coffee?
- I gave it up.
- Wow, didn't you love coffee?
- Things change. People grow.
- So I hear.
- Now, you stop.

Running through my mind is the thought that she seems better than when I knew her. When I knew her, she was desperately seeking attention. Now she seems more at peace with herself and her demons. I say,

- I have to ask. Why did you contact me out of the blue?
- You contacted me.
- What did I say?
- That part was unclear. That's why I'm here.

Damn it. Tammy intercepted my message. Can two people get the same message? My head fills with uncertainty and a bit of disgust.

- Well, Tammy, I met someone. See, we're currently apart from each other. I was trying to send her an energy love letter. I was practicing my talents.
- Hmm, well keep practicing. Although judging from our past, I would think you have that

down by now. Are you sure that's all you were
trying to do?

Nervously, I sip my coffee. It burns my mouth. I blow out
hoping to put out the flames. Tammy hands me a napkin. She
touches my hand as she does. I feel a buzz of energy. It can't be
certain if it's coming or going. I yank my hand back and smirk,

- Thanks. So you're doing well?
- I am. My practice is booming right now.
- What practice is that?
- Don't you remember? I always wanted to open
a medium practice.
- Duh, of course, you did.
- Well, I did. And it's been nothing but great. It
feels like my abilities have grown.
- I've noticed.
- Meaning?

I pull my coffee toward me. My eyes look at Tammy's hands
that are both on the table. Then I look at her eyes and say,

- I sensed it.
- Tell me about this new girl.
- There's nothing really to say except that we
have this undeniable connection, and yet we
can't be together.
- Why not?
- She's with someone.

Tammy grabs my hand.

- Oh my, is she married?

I close my eyes and sip my coffee. Tammy continues,

- You're not that guy. There's plenty of women
out there.
- I know. I just can't help myself. I would do

anything for her.

– You should back off. Find another girl.

– Maybe you're right.

– You think?

I look down, and her hand is on mine. I pull my hand away and grab my coffee. Tammy is glowing. I feel tired and beaten.

– Tammy, I'm not feeling so well. I think I'm
going to go.

– It was fabulous to see you. You'll bounce back,
you always do.

– Thanks. I guess.

– Find a new girl. Will you?

– I'll see you, Tammy.

– Keep that light up, Eddie.

I walk away with my half-full coffee. I'm glad we're not together anymore. I'm ready for a nap.

# 16

## Day 16

I'm going in search of the rapists the old fashion way. I'm hitting the streets. Hopefully, I can pick up on their energy.

I focus on my intention and put it out into the world. It's sometimes tough to do while walking. I stop at the corner and center myself. My arms raise, and my energy connects with the world. While in this meditative state, I put out there what I want. Of course, I say Nora which connects me with the power of love and makes me buzz so good. Then I put out there that finding the rapists is my highest priority.

The sound of people walking around me doesn't distract me. I don't open my eyes. My ability to separate is great. I hear people snicker as they pass. Suddenly, a splash of hot liquid hits my feet. My eyes open. A car speeds away with someone hanging out the window. I hear him say,

– Life coach yourself asshole.

It's one of the kids from jail. Fear takes the place of my positivity. The hair on my neck rises. The kid gives me the finger as the car speeds off. My automatic response is to give them the finger back. The car screeches to a stop. The reverse lights come on. My head darts around in search of safety. Back a block is an alley that won't fit a car because the trash guy is getting the trash. That's my spot.

I run for dear life as the car speeds toward me in reverse. The car is just about to me as I round the corner of the alley. The garbage truck is on the second to last dumpster. I use every ounce of energy to sprint toward it. If I can get around it, then they won't be able to follow. The car speeds to a stop and begins following me with the front. I don't want to look back because I don't want to die. I do anyway. Both of the kids from the jail are in the car. Their eyes are on me. It's as if their mission is to kill me. I didn't even do anything except give them the finger. I hear one of them yell,

– Die, die my darling.

Just as the heat of the motor breathes down my neck, I duck around the garbage truck. The sound of their car slamming to a halt is like music to my ears. I round the corner and duck into the coffee shop. I run straight into the bathroom. Relief and breath slowly come into me as I lean on the locked door.

– Fuck! Why do they have to be such dicks?

I splash water on my face and try to relax. Someone knocks on the door. My panic returns. What do I do? I answer in a lower toned voice,

– Someone is in here.

What if that's them? But they don't know which way I went. What if they got lucky?

– Fuck me.

There is a window in here. It is small and painted shut. It's my only option. I bang on it hoping not to make too much noise. I hear through the door,

– Is everything okay in there?

– I'll be out in a second.

I frantically try to get the window open. It won't budge. The knocking on the door is getting louder.

– If there is ever a time that I need you, God, it's now. Please save me.

My phone begins buzzing in my pocket. It's my mom. We always answer each other's calls. I'm not sure that's possible today. The window finally opens. I climb. It's a tight fit. What choice do I have? My phone rings again. If it's my mom, it must be something important.

– Fuck!

I try my hardest to crawl through the window. My butt isn't fitting. My phone buzzes in my pocket again. I crawl back out of the window just as the door to the bathroom opens. My phone falls as my feet hit the ground. In the doorway is a barista and the black girl I said "damn" to the other day. The look on her face is complete disdain. She says,

– I should have known it would be you.

My eyes glance over her shoulder in search of the hoodlums. They aren't anywhere in sight. I pick up my phone. The black girl's big brown eyes are glaring at me. I smile at her and say as I walk out,

– Stay Golden.

I walk past her. The whole coffee shop is looking at me. I bow to the patrons as I exit. The first thing I do is check my phone. They're three missed calls. One is from my mom. The other two are from Nora. I call Nora back. This could be the moment she says yes to "us." I knew it would happen. She doesn't answer. Her voicemail says her mailbox is full. It's times like these that I want to throw my phone.

I call my mom back.

– Hey, Mom.

- How are you, honey? Long time no talk.

She always says this. It's her way of guilting me for not living in the same city as her. I say,

- I'm good. Same-old, same-old.

- Good. Well, pack your bags. We're going to Florida to see your brother, Nick.

- I know my brother's name. What's the occasion?

- Family needs to see each other once in a while.

- Let me check my schedule.

- Don't you make your schedule?

- People need me when they need me.

- We need you. It has been a year. Book a ticket. I'll pay.

- Florida, here I come.

# 17

## Day 17

The plane ride seemed longer than it should have. Perhaps, it was the small seats of Southwest Airlines. It may have been the drunk people behind me always getting up and using my chair as their handrail. My body aches, and I can use a drink. My legs are stiff but should loosen by the time I get out of this terminal. There stand my mom and step-dad Ray waiting for me with smiling faces. It reminds me of coming back for Christmas break during college. It feels nice to be loved. We have about an hour drive to our time-share hotel. It is right on the beach and has a pool. I nap the whole way.

When we're about twenty minutes away, we stop at a classy seafood restaurant for some well-needed nourishment. I wake just as we pull in.

- Are we there?

My mom says,

- No, honey. We're hungry and thirsty.

Ray says,

- I'm hungry. She's both.

I rub my eyes and say,

- I'm both too.

Mom rubs my leg and smiles at me for our alikeness.

The place is crowded for mid-afternoon which probably means that Ray chose well. He usually does. He loves food almost as much as mom loves wine. Seafood is what I'll be eating this whole Florida trip. Mom orders sea bass. I follow suit. Not because we're that much alike rather because I can't remember the last time I had it. Ray orders the same thing he always orders when we eat seafood. You would think one would get sick of lobster, but he never does. We get a bottle of Pinot Noir because mom prefers red. I would have gone with a white. The Pinot is drinkable. It will do its purpose.

We have the typical conversation while catching up. You know, all about the relatives and such. I don't mention Nora, the rape, the suicide, or going to jail. Those are the things I'm here to forget.

As the alcohol kicks in, all I want to do is talk about my and Nora's connection. I want to find out if that is why my parents got married. Did they feel like this too? Instead, I excuse myself and go to the bathroom. I splash water on my face and stare into my eyes. Nora fills my head. I can feel my tears forcing their way to my eyes. Someone enters. I pretend that I have something in my eye and play with it. I need to come up with a way to mask these feelings.

I sit back at the table and sip my wine. Mom asks,

- Should we get more wine?

- I'm okay. I don't want to fall asleep yet.

Mom asks,

- So do you have a love in your life? Someone
your age should. You aren't getting any younger.
Soon the good ones will all be gone.

I have to look away because my tears are breaking through

my defenses. A sip of wine and the couple arguing on the other side of the dining room bring me back. I say,

– I hope to have something in the works.

Mom says with a mouthful,

– What does that mean?

Ray swallows his lobster bite and says,

– It means he doesn't have anyone.

Mom continues after washing her food down with her wine,

– Is that true? You have no one? That's not good. How do you life coach people if you can't even find a girl?

– Mom, I life coach them just fine. I'll find someone when the time is right.

– Honey, you aren't getting any younger.

She always does this when she gets tipsy. I say,

– I know, Mom. I know.

I take a big sip of my wine. It hurts a little as it goes down. I say,

– Mom did you ever feel like you have a superpower?

Ray coughs his food into his hand. It's like the words out of my mouth are the most ridiculous words ever spoken. He shakes his head and eats the lobster bite again. Mom immediately grabs her wine. Judging by the look in her eyes, she thinks I should be committed. She says,

– Even though we have these powers, God doesn't want us to act upon them because they could be the gateway to Satan.

– I would think that God would want us to shine.

– God wants us to follow his word so we can all find his salvation.

Feeling the wine, I continue,
- Mom, do you believe in energy connection?
- Like a soulmate?
- Sort of, more like two people who are drawn
to each other but they don't know why. They do
know that they are supposed to be together.
Now, do you act on that? Or do you let it pass?
- I'm not sure.
- What if you could communicate with that
person with energy?
Ray says,
- You a psychic?
- No, but what if I can send energy to people?
I'm not saying I can communicate with random
people. What if I could communicate with
people that I have a connection with? For
example, say I like a girl, which needs to
happen more, and all I do is think about her.
My mom says,
- That's not a superpower. That's love.
- Okay, but what if all of a sudden you get a
feeling that something is wrong with that
person, do you call and check on them?
- Of course, you do. That's not a superpower.
That's intuition.
- Okay, but what if you practiced connecting
with that feeling, that energy?
Ray says,
- Are you love sore for a girl?
- Maybe, but what if you practiced getting into
that state where you could have that intuition?

And then you harnessed it.
- Telepathy?
- Perhaps someday with practice. Right now it's
in the early stages.
Ray rolls his eyes and says to my mom,
- Are there life coaches who coach life coaches?
She says,
- Be nice.
I pour the rest of the wine into my glass and say,
- Well, that's what's going on in my world. And I
think that is what makes me a good life coach.
It's the fact that I can radiate like a battery and
people want some of that. With practice, my
power will grow.
My mom pours some of the wine from my glass into hers.
She finishes it and looks at Ray. They don't seem convinced of
my superpower. You would think they would be a little more
understanding of their son's situation instead of thinking he
is a crazy person. I may be crazy, but it doesn't change the fact
that I have a superpower and choose to embrace it. I thought
that they would be happy for me. My mom says,
- On that note, you ready to go?
Ray says,
- Hold on a second. Are you kidding me? A
superpower!? You got some serious problems
kid. For someone your age to say these things
is downright preposterous.
My mom's eyes get wide as she hears this and tries to interject,
- Ray, please.
- No. I've been dealing with his crap for
twenty-two years. When he said he wanted to

be a life coach, I supported him even though I thought it was a bad idea. I mean really, who becomes a life coach but crazy thinking people. You need to get back to reality before it's too late and you end up with nothing. Wake up, Eddie! It's time. This is one of those real-life moments you always talk about. Here's another one, wake up!

My mom says,

– That's a little harsh, honey.

– It needed to be said.

I say,

– Can we go now?

I'm not sure I deserved that. Ray means well. One thing sticks with me as we exit. The fact that my mom said she didn't know if we were supposed to hold onto the special connections that we sometimes feel in life. It almost saddens me to think that she might have passed on one of these connections or that she isn't open to receive. The ride home is a quiet one. When we get to the hotel, everyone goes into their bedrooms, and we say goodnight.

I flop down on the bed. It's hard as a rock. I wipe my eyes and think of ways to keep my parents from thinking that I'm crazy. They always knew I was a little crazy. This time I may have gone too far. Even though too far is the truth. Maybe they weren't ready. Maybe some people aren't ready for change because change is different.

Tomorrow is a new day. I turn off the light. The last words from my mouth are my usual,

– I love you, Nora. Goodnight.

# 18

## Day 18

My older brother Nick and his family come to the hotel to hang at the pool and visit. It seems weird to me because we are at New Smyrna Beach. Why wouldn't you just swim in the ocean? Maybe if you live by the sea, it loses its appeal. It could be because this beach is often on "Shark Week." I don't know if they know that, but I'm not going to bring it up. Nick is three years older than me and is married to Tracey. They've been together for like twenty years or so. Their kids are great. They are eleven, eight, and five. It's great to see them and our day is full of playing at the pool and hot sun. When a lot of people get together, it's hard to connect with anyone.

When the sun goes down, we get some fish po'boy sandwiches from a local food stand. They are surprisingly good. The hippie looking fellow that sells them to us says that his brother catches the fish daily. After we eat, it's time for the big kids to get away. Nick, His wife Tracey, and I hit the streets in search of relief and some real catch-up time.

There's only one street in New Smyrna Beach with bars on it. We go there. We hit the bar that looks to be the most happening. It happens to be the Irish one. Irish bars always seem to have good beers. There are three seats at the bar waiting for us. It's as if they knew we were coming. I order an IPA. My brother and his wife order Bud Light. Bud Light must be a Florida beer. Suppose you have to fight that southern food weight gain somehow.

I tell them that I told our parents I have a superpower. My brother Nick laughs. His wife Tracey wants to hear more. I explained about having energy connections and being able to contact people without words. Of course, Nora comes up. I get all emotional. Why did she have to call me before I left? What did she want? My brother rolls his eyes a lot. He gets that from our step-dad Ray. Tracey seems interested in this connection with Nora. My focus stays on her.

On a side note, when you have a job where you constantly have to listen to people talk, it feels good to get a chance to talk yourself. Evidently, people think I'm self-centered. Honestly, it's just that it's finally my turn to speak.

The whole time Tracey and I are talking, my brother Nick just looks on. When he does talk, all he talks about is how his construction business is finally doing well. My other brother, Eric does heating and air conditioning. He lives in Australia. I'm the black sheep in the family because I'm the only one who doesn't do blue-collar work. I did learn to plumb during my on-again-off-again college time. I life coached myself out of that job real quick.

I don't see Nick more than once every two years. It's great to see him even though he didn't say much about his world. It makes me wonder when people don't say anything about themselves. What are they trying to hide? We drink the night to a close then stumble back to the hotel. It's a ten-minute walk. I don't remember any of it.

# 19

## Day 19

I'm drinking coffee alone in the room. Everyone else is down at the pool swimming. I'm sitting in the kitchen trying to enjoy the fact that I'm with my family at a beachfront hotel.

My second cup of weak coffee that my mom makes isn't doing the job. A shot of tequila is in order. Yesterday when we arrived at the beach, my mom bought a box of wine, and I purchased a bottle of tequila. Just as the shot buzzes my head, there's a knock at the door. It's Tracey.

– Can I come in?

– But, of course.

– How come you aren't at the pool?

– I need a minute to recuperate. How come you aren't?

– I wanted to talk to you.

– Shots first? The first one helped.

Tracy sits at the kitchen table and says,

– No thanks.

– To Family.

Tracey smiles. I slam the shot. It spins my head a bit. It helps me feel that things aren't so bad. Thank you, world, for tequila.

Tracey looks at me and says,

– Can we talk about your situation?

– Sure.

– Nora, is that her name?

– Yeah. What about her?

– You should let that go. For a mother, being there for her kids is the most important thing in life. It doesn't matter if things aren't going well in her marriage. She'll stick it out for her kids.

– But she was the one who initiated it.

– It doesn't matter. The only thing that matters is her children. That's the way it is, and that's the way it will always be. You'll understand when you have kids.

– I guess so. But that doesn't make it any easier for me. And what if she's different?

– Here's an example. Take Nick and me. We have been together for twenty years.

– That's a long time.

– Yeah, he's not the man I married anymore. Now he's a sociopath. He only cares about work and drugs. He doesn't care about me. He doesn't love me anymore. I don't love him anymore either. But we're still together. You know why?

– The kids.

– Exactly. The kids. We're thinking about moving. I'm thinking about a life without him. He's probably thinking the same thing. Sometimes, I think he wants to hit me. It scares me. Living in fear of your husband sucks. And look we're still together. Why?

- The kids.

It's hard to hear that your brother's wife is living in fear of your brother. I pour myself another shot and slam it. I don't offer Tracey one. She continues,

- Exactly. And if someone will live through that, then Nora won't be leaving her family anytime soon. She's no different. No matter how bad it gets for her, she'll always do what is best for her kids.

- I understand. But our connection is so strong.

- Maybe you're the light that gets her through tough situations at home. Maybe that is why you crossed her path. Maybe it wasn't to be lovers but to help each other in their time of need.

- But I want more than that.

- Maybe that's all she can give. Last night you said that she opened you up to your feelings and that you wanted to keep that door open because it hasn't been open in a long time. Maybe that was her purpose. "It's better to have loved and lost than to have never loved at all." You know.

- I know. But it doesn't change the fact that it hurts.

- If I were you, I would take this opportunity to find someone. And do it quickly before the door closes, and you become a "Stepford Wife" again.

- I don't want anyone else.

- She's out there. You just have to find her. And I'm not talking about Nora.

– I know. There's more than one person for everyone.

Tracey turns to me and looks me in the eye. She says,

– How good are you at forgetting?

– I'm pretty good.

– Will you forget our conversation about me and your brother? Remember the other parts.

– I will. What were we talking about again?

– Exactly. And you don't want Nora. She cheated to go out with you which means she'll do it again. And this time, it could be on you. Are you coming to the pool?

– Thanks for this. I'll meet you down there in a minute.

Tracey leaves. As soon as the door closes, I say out loud,

– Seriously? She's scared for her well being.

At the pool, Tracey is her usual talkative self. She's talking with my parents and interacting with her kids like everything is hunky-dory. Knowing what I know now, damn she's a good actor. I sit in a beach chair and don't talk much. My mom asks what is wrong. I say,

– I don't usually drink like that. I'm feeling it.

All I can think about is that Tracey could be right. I'm not talking about my brother either. I'm talking about Nora.

I try to find a comfortable spot to sleep in this hard as a rock bed. It seems like an impossible task. I decide to Facebook message Nora. To my surprise, she texts me back. I say,

: Howdy Ponygirl.

: How are you?

: I'm okay. I'm in Florida visiting family. Why

did you call me a few days ago?

: I got a bad feeling and wanted to know if you were okay.

: I am having a bit of a hard spell. That's why I'm in Florida.

: Anything I can do?

: You could visit me. Haha.

: I've been to Florida, hated it.

: It's like another country down here. Where I'm at, it's very backwoods.

: I had these adamant vibes about you. It made me nervous, so I called.

I smile and type,

: I miss you too.

: Please don't start that. You know we aren't supposed to be talking.

: I can't help but think about you all the time.

: I have to go... I think about you too... A little too often.

: You make me smile. Stay Golden Ponygirl.

# 20

## Day 20

Something is missing when I wake. The feeling of loss that has been haunting me since Nora went away is gone. What was it about last night that changed that? It must have been talking with Tracey and her making it clear to me the truth of the situation. Maybe it's that Nora, and I are in this together. The fact that Nora too is having a hard time dealing with "us" is validation for the way I'm feeling. It's validation that we did have something undeniable.

Today, I'm driving to my dad's house. He lives inland about one hour down the same road. I turn twice and then I'm there. He lives in a podunk town called Eustis. My half-sister Sam, who lives with him, calls it Useless. I'm so excited to see them. I don't see them but once every two years. Sam and I have the same birthday. It's two weeks from now. We'll be drinking to celebrate. Although, drinking like I did with my brother isn't an option.

I stop at a store and buy my dad a bottle of scotch. He likes single malts, but all I can afford is blended. I get him Monkey Shoulder. In my opinion, it's one of the better blends. It's way better than a Johnny Walker. We drink and catch up. The beautiful thing about parents is whether they were around or not, the connection is always there.

By the time Sam arrives, dad and I have a hearty buzz. She lights up the room as she enters. She is beautiful. Her hair is sun bleached blonde. Her skin is Florida tanned. Her eyes shine blue lightness everywhere they point. She's a twenty-two-year-old hottie. Her aura radiates positivity. It's very alluring. Surely, she'll go far in life. It makes me wonder if she too is a positivity battery. We hug hello. I offer her a drink, but she doesn't like scotch. She has a bottle of Bacardi rum. She makes herself a drink and joins us.

- Let me see that bottle?

Sam hands me the bottle of rum. I put my hand over the top of the bottle to feel its energy. Almost instantly, my head goes numb.

- Yep, I'm allergic.

Dad responds first,

- Those are some psychic powers you got there.

Sam joins in,

- You can tell if you're allergic by holding your hand over something?

- Yes, I can. As I get older, it seems like I've become more in touch with my powers. I think everyone has a superpower.

- If you have one, then I probably have one being born on the same day.

Dad says,

- Not only were you born on the same date, you were born at the same time. Your Grandma Sis was also born on the same date and same time

73

of 530 p.m.

All I can think to say is,

– Wow. Really?

Sam says,

– How come you never told me?

Dad says,

– That's probably why you two are so similar.

I slug my drink and hope she's not totally like me. Although, if she too has this superpower, two superheroes are better than one. I say,

– I think I have a superpower other than telling
what I'm allergic to. It seems as if I can send
messages through energy. And sometimes, it is
kind of like I'm a battery of light which isn't
always good 'cause people try to steal it. For a
while, I was working on moving inanimate
objects, but I gave that up. Maybe I'll try again
'cause my powers seem closer to the surface.

Dad responds first,

– You might. My mom said she did.

Sam says,

– Does that mean I do too?

Dad and I both say,

– You might.

I continue,

– You don't think that is weird, me saying that
stuff?

– Everyone has one thing they can do better than
anybody. Maybe that's yours. Maybe that's why
you're a good life coach.

Sam says,

– I love it. It's positively lovely. You know,
people tell me I'm a ray of sunshine. And
sometimes I feel like I am. Like I can go into a
place and make it brighter.
– I bet you can.
Dad says,
– She does have that ability. I've seen it.
A smile fills my face. I say,
– I love you guys.
They both say back,
– I love you too.
I ask,
– Can we group hug?
Without any hesitation, we do. A vibration fills my body. The same positive vibration that fills me when I'm connecting to send messages. It feels good. Before letting go, I ask,
– Do you feel that?
Sam says,
– I do.
Dad says,
– I love you guys.


Florida was a good idea. The family is such a nice change to see. I love them all. Seeing them brought a feeling of goodness that I don't want to shake. Perhaps, a new door is opening.

# 21

# Day 21

My first order of business is to get my life back in order. While sipping coffee, I check my messages. It says my mailbox is full which is very exciting. Could I be back in business? The first message is from Eva. She's the woman who called the cops on me and said I was a peeping Tom. She wants to make an appointment. The next message is from Eva. She wants to make an appointment. The third message is from Eva. This time, she yells at me to pick up the phone like I can hear her message on one of those old-time answering machines. Here is what she said:

"Damn it, Eddie. You're supposed to be my life coach. Where are you? I need you. I know you can hear this. Pick up the damn phone. Pick up, damn it."

I start skipping a few messages as I realize that she has filled my entire voicemail. Here's another one:

"You son-of-a-bitch, pick up. You're never here when I need you. Get your ass over here. Get over here now. NOW, Goddamn it! As your patient, I order you to get over and tend to me."

Her voice becomes soft spoken on her last message. She whimpers:

"Please come over, coach...Please."

I call. Eva doesn't answer. I leave a message,

– Hey, Eva, this is Life Coach Eddie. I was out of town and just got back. I see that you called a few times or should I say quite a few. It's 930 a.m. I'm coming over.

I don't look around. I knock on the front door. Eva answers as if she was waiting by the door. She's wearing a flower covered silk robe. Her blonde hair is messy like bed head. I would say she looks pretty good but don't have time to think because she immediately pulls me into her embrace. She squeezes and kisses me like I'm her long lost love. Resistance is futile. Our lips break apart long enough for me to say,

– Is everything okay?

– It is now. I love you so much.

– Are you going to call the cops again?

She drops her robe to the floor displaying her near perfect body in all of its glory. Her breasts hang perfectly. It's like gravity doesn't apply to her. Her stomach is tight like she's been working out. I say,

– I guess that answers that.

She rubs her tight body against mine, and it gets me going. It's hard to resist a beautiful naked woman who wants nothing but you. This time, I pull her close. She moans like she's having an orgasm. In the heat of passion, she cries out,

– Hold me. Hold me.

I'm glad she can't see my face because my eyes just rolled. She pushes my face into her sweet D-cups. They fill my mouth, and all is forgotten. Until she says,

- Tell me you love me.

Hearing this stops my embrace. But Eva is too ready to resist. My mouth sucks on her neck hoping she didn't just say that. She says,

- Say that you love me.

My mouth moves back to her nipple. With a mouth full, I say,

- Eva, you're pure gold.

She pushes me away to look in my eyes. She says,

- Why won't you say it again?

- Say what?

- That you love me? You said that you loved me.

So, say it.

The only thing going through my head is how hot she is. I pull her close to continue our embrace. She stops it and looks me in the eye. My little head takes over. I say,

- Eva baby, I love everything about you.

I yank her back in hoping she'll take that as an answer. I breathe my warm breath on her neck while kissing it ever-so-softly. She's about to say something then her head tilts to the side, her fingers run through my hair, and she lets out an orgasmic size moan. Her nails dig into my back which makes me moan back. She says,

- Say it again.

She has me too hot to resist her demands. I say,

- I love Eva.

- Again.

- I love Eva.

- Again.

Her body is gyrating with emotion. With each answer, she gets hotter. We get hotter.

- Say it.

– I love you, Eva.

She throws me down on the ground and mounts me like a horse. Her beautiful body begins thrusting back and forth riding my hard cock. It feels spectacular. I close my eyes. She says,

– Say it again.

– I love you, Nora.

She thrusts her body off of mine. My eyes open when she slaps me in the face and says,

– Who the fuck is Nora?!

– Did I say, Nora? I meant Eva. Come back over here, baby. I love you, Eva. I love you. I don't even know a Nora. I used to. But I don't now. Eva, please come back over here.

– Fuck you. Get out before I call the cops.

With lightning speed, my clothes are on, and I am out. At the door, I turn and say,

– Eva, I'm here for you.

She picks up the closest projectile and hurls it at me. It happens to be her coffee cup. It hits the wall beside my head and crumbles. That's my cue. I speed-walk to my car and don't look back. In the rearview mirror, I look at myself and say,

– You dumb mother fucker. Crazy is as crazy does.

My foot slams on the accelerator. The tires peel out.

My next stop is for some coffee. It's about noon, so there's a line. Young folks wake up late. While I'm waiting in line, the same black girl that seems to plague me here walks in. She is smiling with her cellphone glued to her face. When she hangs up, her face lights up like a Christmas tree. Good for her. It reminds me that I just got laid. It may have been a crazy person, but I still got some action.

The black girl's eyes and mine meet. Her demeanor immediately changes. It goes from Christmas to the day after New Year's day. I smile and turn away. Why am I acting like this? Why am I not following my Stay Golden philosophy? Who benefits from our so-called feud? It only hurts myself if I continue to focus on it.

The barista says,

– Next.

It's my turn to order. I get out of line and stand behind the black girl. Her face snarls. She says,

– What do you want?

– Hi. My name is Eddie. What's yours?

– None of your business, freak.

– Wow. I never heard that name before. It has a nice ring to it. "None Of Your Business Freak."

– What are you going to do now rob the place?

Oh my, God, you are.

She begins looking around in a panic. I say,

– I'm not going to do anything. I just wanted to apologize and introduce myself, so you don't think I'm a freak. You have to admit that our dealings have been unique.

– Uh-huh.

– At the very least you have a story to tell your friends. Honest, I'm harmless and kind of exciting at the same time. It's a weird phenomenon, but it happens. I'm proof. No? Nothing? Can we start over? I'm Eddie.

She doesn't say anything. She just looks at me with her big brown eyes. They seem gigantic when they are glaring at you.

She says,

    – Monica.

    – Hi, Monica, it's a pleasure to meet my coffee shop adversary finally.

She glares at me. Her defenses go back up. I say,

    – Not anymore. Hopefully, we could be coffee shop buddies. Maybe wave at each other and make sure the other is having a good day by passing positivity with a smile.

    – That would be okay.

    – I knew you weren't so bad.

    – What's that supposed to mean? Is that how I come off?

    – Absolutely not. Honestly, you can't blame people for how they act in those strange occurrences. Some say that is who we truly are. I would say that their environment sometimes sways people.

    – Stop right there before you put your foot in your mouth. I don't need your services.

    – I get it. I haven't given the best first impression. But let me assure you, I am happy to meet you. And I only have good intentions toward all things.

    – It's nice to meet you coffee buddy, Eddie. Maybe we can talk another time. Right now, I have to get to work.

    – It's a pleasure to meet you finally, Monica. I'm glad we could clear the air.

    – Is that what we did?

She turns to order. A feeling of defeat runs through my body.

She orders a large coffee with no room. A smile covers my face as I say,

– That's the same thing I order.

She smirks at me like so what. I say to Monica,

– Let me get this.

I order the same thing. Monica says,

– This is a good start. Thank you.

– It's the least I can do.

– Also, thank you for the excitement. My life isn't all that extraordinary.

– Oh, stop. You're just saying that so I don't feel like a freak.

– I'm not. I'll see you around. I'm sure.

– Did you ever eat a fortune cookie and get a good fortune?

– Most of the time they're stupid.

– I got one that I'm supposed to spread to everyone. Don't ask me how I know this, I just do. Here it is: "You will bring sunshine into someone's life."

– That's a good one.

– It's for you too.

Today was a good day. I felt a little.

# 22

# Day 22

Did you ever feel like you woke up on the wrong side of the bed? That's how it feels today. I'm going to center myself and try to keep the vibe from yesterday going. I have to go to the motorcycle shop. I need some positivity for that.

First, some breathing exercises to relax and focus. My preference is to do this standing outside. That way the power of the sun can beat down on me. I concentrate on the feeling of energy running through my body. My hands begin to tingle. Then my body follows suit. When this happens, I have connected with my internal energy. It means I'm connecting with the energy that makes all things. Next, a chant of positivity to make sure my vibration is flowing positively.

- I'm the manifestation of love.

I'm the manifestation of light.

I am Golden Love.

I repeat this until my inner energy begins to flow with Golden Love. Sometimes it's quick but not always. Today, it happens within five minutes. I send out my Golden Love energy for the world. I usually say:

- I love you, Nora.

Her name reminds me to be open and that in order to receive, I must first give. I will always freely give her my love. I send love to my family and friends. When I feel open to receive, I release the energy of that which I want. Today, I want my motorcycle fixed. I focus on that. I repeat everything until my vibration tells me that the energy was received. Once the energy is received, my internal energy begins to flow in a purely positive manner. Golden Love fills me. Now my day will be approached with positivity and love.

When I get to the motorcycle shop, there isn't any free parking, so I park at a meter. My car usually has coins in it. I must have used them on my last laundry day. A quarter is all I can find. This shouldn't take long. An eerie vibration runs through me as I walk. I remind myself that I am Golden Love. Repeating this over and over should help me handle this correctly. When entering the bike filled yard, my bike instantly finds my eye. It is sitting against the wall without a gas tank. I think,

– Those mother fuckers. Stay Golden, Stay Golden...

My direction turns toward my bike. One of the mechanics says,

– Can't you read? No customers allowed.

– That's my bike.

– Oh.

He says this with a complete "oh shit" tone and walks into the office. His actions make me nervous. On the ground beside the bike is the gas tank. It has a giant dent on the side. I pick it up and hold it in my arms like it's my dead baby. Everything else seems to be in order. I'm no mechanic. For all I know, the whole bike could be fucked up.

The worker returns with the manager. The manager is a short white guy that looks about forty. His face is full of concern like that of a lot older of a man. Either he has had a hard life, or I'm in for some bad news. Inside my head, I repeat,

    – I am the manifestation of love,

I am the manifestation of light.

The manager greets me with a handshake. His hand is grease covered. It's probably permanent from years of service. He says,

    – Hi, are you Eddie?

    – Yep.

    – I'm the one you talked to on the phone.

    – Sorry about that. You know, bad news
sometimes breeds bad reactions.

    – You should be more careful.

    – I should be more careful? What about my tank?

    – As I said before, accidents happen. Our policy
is that we aren't responsible for bikes left in the
yard.

    – Left in the yard? I hired you to fix it. It wasn't
left here. You were fixing it.

    – That's your word against ours. See, the way I
see it is that I called and said your bike was
ready and you didn't pick it up.

    – That's fucking bullshit, and you know it.

    – Is it?

    – Why would you fucking do this? You broke it,
and you should fix it. That's what people do.
That's what real businesses do.

    – Sir, please take your bike and leave. There will

be no charge for the carbs. We tuned them, and
they're good. You will need to clean them real
soon. The bike will run but not so good.
- Seriously? WHAT THE FUCK!

Everyone in the shop stops and moves behind the manager.
It looks like they're a gang. They're all dressed the same and
united for one cause. That cause being my destruction. A pit in
my stomach opens. My head begins to drip sweat. I say,
- Surely, we can work this out like gentlemen. I
never wanted any trouble. I just wanted my
bike fixed.
- I know. But there's a certain way to interact
with people on business matters. You don't
threaten them!
- I'm sorry if you thought that was a threat. Like
I said it was just a slight overreaction. I'm sorry.
Can you please fix my bike?
- No. We reserve the right to refuse service. The
sign is right there.
- REALLY?

He says nothing. He just nods. The guys behind him look like
they want me to make a move. It would totally make their day if
I did. My eyes look at my bike. My positivity is now gone. Rage
is taking its place. It takes all that I have to remain civil as these
guys fuck me in the ass.
- Can I pick it up tomorrow? Then I can get a
truck, and I won't ever come back. I won't say
anything bad. I promise. Because you're right.
This is my fault. Please, can we handle this like
men?

The manager sizes me up with his eyes. The mechanics are

still staring at me with a look of death. My eyes turn to my bike with sadness. I say,

- I love that bike.
- Pick it up tomorrow by noon, or we'll put in on the street.
- Thank you so much.
- I don't want to see you around here after that...
Ever.
- Yes, sir.

The manager yells,

- Everyone back to work.

My hands rub my dripping head. Then they rub my bike. I leave the shop with my head down. I make sure not to make eye contact with anyone. Starting out the day with a loss sucks, especially when it's your favorite possession. As soon as I get around the corner, I say to myself,

- Fucking dicks. I should fucking get a gun and fuck those mother fuckers up!

When I get to my car, there's a parking ticket on it. My watch says that I'm five minutes late.

- Fuck me!!!

Coffee was next on my list but not anymore. A real drink is in order. It takes a while to find a free parking space. It's "Mary Weathers" the local dive bar. It's the only one around. The interior is the same as it was two years ago. It's a narrow bar. It's only big enough for the bar and the stools. There is barely enough room to walk to the bathroom. I don't use the bathroom here because it lives up to the dive bar standard. The toilet looks to be from the seventies and probably has never had a cleaning. The ring inside the toilet has moved from brown to black.

The bar itself has walls covered with 1970's paneling and a wood bar that complements it well. This place is always dark. It's probably so the patrons can hide from themselves. Today, which is likely to be the same as every day, the bar is riddled with old-timers sitting alone at the bar. It's weird that no one is talking to anyone. Maybe I came at a lull. The bartender is a short Asian woman who is also the owner. She greets me like she knows me. I can't be certain if she remembers me or she is excellent at her job. My smile returns her greeting along with,

– I'll have a double whiskey on the rocks and a Bud.

As she walks away to pour the drink and my beer, I say,

– I see the place hasn't changed much.

– Honey, this place hasn't changed since 1972, when I bought it.

– That's probably good for business.

– They always know what they're getting.

She sets the drinks in front of me. I raise my glass and say,

– To knowing what you'll get. And to knowing what they'll get.

A wicked smirk fills my face as the double shot fills me with comfort and ideas. I say,

– Can I have another? If you only knew the day I'm having.

She fills my glass and says,

– You look old enough that I don't have to remind you about acting responsibly.

– No, Ma'am. I am as responsible as they come. I'm a life coach.

– Are you the life coach that killed that girl?

The double shot quickly makes its way into my belly. Half of my beer follows suit. I look at her and say,

- I didn't kill her. My technique doesn't work for everyone. It didn't work on her, and she blamed me for her life-ending decision.
- Why do you think someone would want to kill themselves?
- Lots of reasons.
- Yeah, but isn't there usually one that pushes to do it?
- Depression is a powerful thing.
- Yeah. But still, to die at such a young age? Something must have caused that.
- Me. I couldn't help her. Can I have one more? A single this time?
- Honey, be careful.
- I know what I'm doing.

She looks me in the eyes. I look back like I'm attempting to pass a sobriety test. She sets the drink in front of me and says,

- Last one, honey.

I slam my fist on the bar and slam the shot. When the shot is down, everyone in the bar is looking at me. I say,

- What are you looking at?

The bartender comes over and says to me,

- Act responsibly. You said.
- How am I supposed to act responsibly when I just got bent over and fucked up the ass? How am I expected to take that? Am I just supposed to lie down and take it?

One of the customers sitting at the bar says,

- It depends if you liked it.
- I ain't no homo. And I was using a metaphor. Duh.

Another voice says,
- You look like you could be.
- Who said that? Do you want a piece of this?
I'll show you what getting fucked up the ass
feels like after I bash your head in.
The bartender rushes over and takes my beer.
- You got to go, honey. You go now. Get out.
- You brought it up. Fine. I got some bashing to
do. Fuck y'all.
A car almost runs me over during my stumble across the street.
My finger instantly goes up. I say,
- Fuck you mother fucker! Learn how to drive
douche.
The car slams on its breaks. It peels out in reverse and stops
right in front of me. I say,
- Can I help you mister bad driver?
- You best watch where you're walking. And
shut your mouth. You don't know who you're
talking to.
- I think I do, a bad driving douche who thinks
he's tough.
The guy slams his car into park and gets out of the car. He's
about four inches taller than me and clearly enjoys working out.
His shirt sleeves can barely contain his biceps. He was right
when he said I didn't know who I'm fucking with. He says,
- Say it again. I fucking dare you.
- Fuck you.
- Fuck me? Fuck you.
Suddenly, the impact of his fist on my face knocks me down.
He stands over me like Mr. T in "Rocky" and says,
- And stay down if you know what's good for

you.

If this were a cartoon, birds would be flying around my head chirping. My hand rubs the side of my face where he hit me. There's no blood, but there sure is some pain. My eyes look up at him. The look on his face is death. My body rolls back onto the ground. My head slams onto the concrete, and everything goes dark.

When I come to, I'm on the grass beside the sidewalk. The place where dogs always poop. My hand lands in some. Luckily for me, it's dried up.

I'm not quite sure how I got here. It probably looks like I passed out. That's probably why no one bothered to help me. And it's dark out. It makes me wonder how long I've been here. Maybe the bartender can answer some questions. When I walk back in, everyone looks at me. The bartender yells,

– Oh no, you don't. You not allowed in here. Go now.

– Can you tell me what happened first?

– You were threatening people, now go. Don't come back.

What a bitch. There's a liquor store around the corner. A bottle of something should make my head feel better. I say to myself or anyone listening,

– I don't need no stinking bar. I don't need fucking no one.

Some composure gathering is in order before entering the liquor store. It must have worked because the guy sells me a bottle of Jim Beam without even batting an eye. Two giant swigs are my reward for acting sober enough to buy alcohol. My head begins to numb, but my face still hurts. A soothing feeling that only alcohol gives me fills my body. Nora does too but fuck her.

My care level drops enough to live with the pain. There's a park two blocks down. It'll be a perfect place to settle myself.

In the park is a four person swing-set. The middle swing is where my butt plants. Back and forth, I go.

  - Fuck that bar. Fuck that girl. Fuck, everyone! (repeat)

The bottle rewards this genius thinking. While trying to put the cap on, the bottle falls. I follow. Somehow I manage to land on my feet. I must have this drinking thing down. Only a little leaks out of the bottle. Thank God. A swig rewards my valiant rescue effort.

While swinging, I see a little kid across the street. He is throwing buckets of water onto the plants that surround his backyard. His dad sneaks out. The child doesn't see him. He too is carrying a bucket of water. I want to yell to help the kid. It's probably better just to watch and let them have their fun. The dad sneaks up behind him and just as the boy throws the water on the plants. The father throws water on the kid. The child screams. The dad runs around the yard trying to keep away from his son's wet wrath.

The child fills his bucket and chases his father. He throws water and misses. The dad fills his bucket and throws water and hits the kid. The child screams again. The mom comes out the back door and tells them to settle down. Just as she does, the boy soaks the dad with a bucket of water. The mom winks at the kid then goes back inside the house. It's fun to watch their family play together. Someday, I'll get to do that. Throwing buckets of water on each other would be fun.

  - I'll throw buckets of water on the motorcycle
shop. Those assholes.

Just as I say this, a paint truck drives past.

Even though it's dark outside, I'm wearing sunglasses in the hardware store. The brightest color green will do. Think Incredible Hulk green on steroids. My sunglasses are necessary just to look at the color sample on the lid. This color will be perfect. The clerk comments as I pay,

- That is one bright color.

I smile and nod. Saying something might give away the fact that intoxication fills me. The clerk continues,

- You know, green is the color of change?

- Things are going to change. That's for sure.

- What are you painting?

- A bike.

- You should probably get an oil based paint if you're doing that. It won't come off in the rain.

- I'm kinda in a hurry.

- Are you alright? You sound out of it?

- I'm just buying paint. It's not like I'm going to do anything with it. I gotta go. Can I get the paint or not?

He looks me in the eyes. Through my sunglasses, I watch as he thinks about it. He reluctantly takes my money. My wallet falls as I put the change away. I hear him say,

- Next. Can you move along, sir?

My hand grabs the paint with a fist. I turn to the clerk and say,

- Fuck you.

He yells,

- Security!

I hustle out the door and don't look back.


About a block away from the motorcycle shop is where I stop

to gather myself. The hood of my sweatshirt disguises my head, along with the sunglasses. My hands vigorously shake the paint up. My keys are barely strong enough to pry the lid open. I set the paint down and begin jumping up and down to get loose.

– You sure about this? Fuck 'em. They deserve
everything coming to them. You can still back
out. Fuck it. It's go time.

With each step, my trashed bike flashes in my head. With each step, it becomes easier for me to do what I'm about to do. When I'm within a house of the bike yard, the paint lid comes off. My approach becomes more stealth like a ninja. A bit of recon is in order. The paint can sits in the bushes while I investigate the attack zone. It's all clear. Not a worker in sight. I swirl the paint around by twisting the can. Some of it spills onto my shoe. The damp grass helps wash it off.

– You sure about this? Fuck 'em.

My hand clenches the can. My head stays down. Not a car in sight. Nothing is moving anywhere around me. It's now or never. Heave. The paint flies out of the can and onto the bikes. The only word to describe it is,

– Whoa.

Each splatter puts a smile on my face. I make sure to move around to ensure that every single bike in the yard has paint on it.

– Serves you right fuckers!

I give the yard the finger then high-tail it out of there. It's trash day tomorrow, so I dispose of the can in a nearby trash can. The adrenaline running through my body sobers me up like getting hit by a right hook would. It's a feeling I haven't felt in a while. Not the right hook but rather the adrenaline. My walk to the car is electric. This must be how real redemption feels.

I sleep good tonight.

# 23

## Day 23

I feel surprisingly good considering the day I had yesterday. The warm water of the bathroom sink splashes on my face. A fresh feeling fills me. I scrub the remainder of the paint off of my hands. It feels more like blood than paint. That could be because I watch movies.

I don't need a coffee to get moving today. I do need a U-Haul. They say they'll have a pick-up truck ready, but I better be on time because they're getting a lot of orders today.

The U-Haul place is full of biker types. Everyone is trying to rent a truck. If I didn't know what was going on, I would be genuinely concerned.

The first thing to catch my eye at the motorcycle shop is all of the News trucks. This is a big deal in our quiet little town. I find an unmetered spot down the street. It's more of a walk, but that's fine. A well-dressed female reporter approaches me as I walk up. I recognize her from TV. She's not my favorite, but she's cute.

- Hi, sir. Can I ask you a few questions?
- Sure.

She signals to the camera guy. He rolls the camera. She switches into her reporter's voice and says,

- How do you feel about your bike and the
  whole bike yard being vandalized?
- What happened is a monstrosity to the
  community. Whoever did this should be
  punished to the full extent of the law. My bike
  was inside when I was here yesterday.
  Hopefully, it still is. I love that bike.

Almost every bike in the yard has paint on it. I want to smile and say serves you right, but I don't. People are screaming at any shop worker they can find. It's hard to hide my smile knowing that they'll have to pay for everyone's bike to be cleaned and when that doesn't work, they'll have to buy people new bike parts. I look around for my bike. It's not where it was yesterday. My eyes survey the yard in hopes that it isn't here. There are a few bikes that are so paint covered that it's hard to make out what kind they are. I get a closer look.

- Mother fucker!

My bike is completely green. It's almost unrecognizable with it's dented tank and Incredible Hulk coloring. I wait my turn to yell at the manager. There are twelve people in front of me. A mechanic emerges from the office and calls for the manager. The manager is busy trying to calm the angry pack. He heads inside. People are angrily stirring. Some people are talking to each other. Others are hovering over their bike. I keep to myself. The guy in front of me won't stop grumbling angry threats. I can't see his face. But judging by the energy he's giving off, I don't want to. He says to the guy beside him,

- This shit makes me want to kill someone. Grab
  that fucker by the neck and say die, die my

darling. Then choke the life out of him. He'll be
screaming, and I'll be smiling as I take his every
breath away.

The guy he's talking to says,

– I love my bike too, but damn.

When I hear "die, die my darling," fear shoots through my
body like an arrow would a rabbit. Silent panic fills me. I lower
my hat and attempt to get out of there. Leaving is harder than
expected when there are a bunch of motorcycles blocking yours
in. The only way out is to go forward then go around. If I do that,
he'll see me for sure. The manager emerges from the office. He
yells to everyone,

– Listen up. We just watched security camera
footage and caught the whole thing on video.

Without looking up, I slowly move my bike. I'm right behind
the kid that wants to kick my ass. Without looking at him, I say,

– Excuse me.

– You ain't waiting to see what happens.

– I gotta go.

The manager continues,

– Not to worry folks, once we process the video,
we should be able to see the perps face and this
whole thing will be resolved. We'll get all of
your bikes as good as new.

His words stop me in my tracks. Sweat pours down my face
as panic consumes me. The only thing to do is get out of there.
By mistake, I bump the kid's bike who wants to beat me up. He
responds,

– Watch what you're doing dick head.

– Sorry man.

– Do I know you?

- I don't think so.
- I think I do. In fact, I know I do. You're the fucking life coach.
- Look, man, we're all victims here. I just want to get my bike and go home.
- I don't think so, partner.
- Seriously? What the fuck did I do?
- You know what the fuck you did. You remember jail?
- Please leave me alone.

While attempting my quick getaway, I bump over two bikes. One of them knocks over a barrel of water. It soaks the fallen bikes and quickly turns green. Someone yells,

- Look, it's coming off.

Now is my chance to sneak my bike out. The kid doesn't follow. I can't believe the paint came off that easy.

- Goddamn it.

I hustle my bike up the street and to the truck. It's quite difficult to push a 500-pound bike up a ramp and into a truck all by yourself. As I push, it suddenly gets easier. The bike is on the truck. Now I can get out of here. I turn to thank the person that helped me out, and it's the kid. He's standing there with a devilish grin as his fist greets my face. It knocks me back and wakes me up at the same time. I'm able to kick him off but only after he delivers two more punches to the side of my head. My kick sends him flying off the back of the truck. I run like there's no tomorrow.

Cheering fills the street which gets me to look back. Everyone at the motorcycle shop is screaming. It sounds like a victory party. While looking back, I'm greeted by an airborne body. The kid lands on top of me. We roll into a trash can. Trash flies everywhere. The green paint can rolls onto the ground. Punches begin to bombard my head. I try to dodge them, but there are too many. My hand reaches around for a weapon of some sort. The paint can is within reach. I swing it and hit him right on the side of the head. This blow momentarily stops his punches. He scowls at me like now it's my time to die. I swing it again and this time nail him right in the temple. The hit knocks him off of me. His body falls to the ground. I can't help but hit him again.

   – You fucking fuck! How do you like it?

His body begins to twitch. I say,

   – Die, die my darling!

I kick him in the stomach. His body doesn't move. The ground beside his head looks like Christmas. It's full of green paint and red blood. I inspect the paint can. It says indoor water-based paint. I chuck the can into the empty trash can. It dawns on me that the kid isn't moving. I check for a pulse. There isn't one.

   – Fuck! Fuck! Fuck!

I survey the area, and no one is around to see what just happened.

   – What do I fucking do? Fuck me.

I try to put his body in the trash can. He's heavier than he looks. People are walking toward me. My adrenaline gives me a boost of strength. I get his feet into the can and put the lid on it just as the people are close enough to see what I'm doing. I kick some of the trash over the blood and act like I'm dealing with the spill. One of the people walking says,

   – Don't know if you heard but the paint is water-
   based and washes right off with a power
   sprayer.

   – Is that what that screaming is?

- Stupid-ass vandals.

They keep walking. I wipe the sweat and the paint from my brow.

- Goddamn it!

I sit on the trash can and contemplate my next move. My shoes have paint and blood all over them. They too look like Christmas. I wipe them in the grass. It gives the grass a blueish color.

I hustle back to the truck. My feet seem clean enough not to be obvious or leave a paint trail. I strap in my bike. Another passer-by says,

- If you take your bike back, they'll water blast
the paint off for you.

- Thanks, but I'm in a hurry.

The guy who just passed is walking toward the trash can. Sweat pours down my face. He has an empty fast food bag in his hand that he probably wants to throw away. I run as fast as I can toward the can. I jump right in front of it and sit on it. I say,

- Hi.

- Could you move so I can throw this away?

- I could. I'd rather not. I rather talk to you.

- What are you gay or something? I ain't fucking
interested queer.

He throws the bag. It hits me in the face. He walks off. He looks back. I wave at him and smile. He gives me the finger and continues. I hustle back to the truck and drive it right beside the trash can. I attempt to put it in the back of the truck. The lid falls off, and his arm comes out. I get it back in before anyone notices. A guy that is walking offers some assistance. Two people picking it up is easier than one. The man says,

- That's some serious trash.

– It sure is.

The guy walks away. I strap the can in and get the hell out of there.

Everyone looks at me as I pass the News trucks. Goosebumps cover my body. Some people point me to the yard. I wave as sweat drips from my brow. My fear turns to adrenaline as I make it to the main street. It rushes through me like a river in the spring. It doesn't feel like a punch in the face. It feels more like I just went skydiving. The energy buzz makes my whole body tingle. I don't even get this feeling when I connect with Nora. I scream with delight,

– Whew!!

First stop is my place to unload the bike. The next thing is to figure out what to do with the body. The trash can contains it well. It doesn't smell yet. The energy running through me is like that of a little kid about to see Santa Claus for the first time. It makes everything I do seem effortless. Even lifting the can out of the truck is easy. I can't help but jump up and down. Sitting still cannot happen right now. I even do some push-ups and sit-ups. Goddamn, it feels good to be alive.

After the body is in the corner of the garage and the bike is down, it's time to hose my bike off. The water handle is on full blast. I spray away. The paint drips right off. Green water covers the driveway. A little bit of red comes off of my shoes and washes into the grass as well. Whatever green paint doesn't come off, I scrub with a brush. With some work, it all comes off.

I spray the driveway clean and relive the fight inside my head. First, it's his punches to my head. Then it's me doing whatever I can to dodge his hits. The feeling of the paint can in my hand is the best feeling of all. It makes me clench a fist. I smile. In my head, I hear him say,

   – Die, die my darling.

I relive the swing over and over again. With a scowl of delight, I repeat,

   – Die, die my darling!

My hand unclenches and my body freezes. "Die, die my darling!" I've heard that before. He and his friend said it to me in jail. I've also heard it one other time. It's what the rapist said to the girl. It did happen. Does that mean I killed the rapist? Does that mean I did something good? I turn to the body-filled trash can and say,

   – Fuck you dick! I did the world a favor. You
   raped Mary Levitt and caused her to kill herself?
   And I killed you. That makes me a real-life
   hero. I'm a real hero in every sense of the word.
   Eddie, the hero. Which also makes me an even
   bigger target if the other guy finds out that I
   killed his friend. Fuck. I need a drink.

The local dive-bar is where I find myself. It's dark and empty. It looks the same as last time I was in here a day ago. Two old guys are sitting at the corner of the bar. They are playing a card game while enjoying their drinks. The same bartender is working. She gives me the evil eye. I immediately sit. She walks over to me. Her walk is that of an owner. Or rather, that of someone whose law rules this place. She says,

   – No Funny business. You hear me?

   – I'm so sorry about the other day. My life has
   been crazy lately. I swear I'll be good. I
   promise.

- No shots for you.
- A beer?
- Only beer.
- Thank you. That sounds great.

She slides me a beer. I slide her the cash. It's not a shady transaction, but for some reason, it feels like one. When the beer touches my lips, it tastes so good. It's as if this is my first sip of liquid after a ten-mile hike through the desert. The only thing that would be better than this beer is someone to share it with. I wish I could tell someone what happened. Then everything could go back to the way it was.

Things were good back then. Back then, being twenty-five days ago. Nora and I were together. Everything seemed to be clicking. Now, everything appears to be changing. I'm uncertain about my career, living here, why I'm still alone, and if the other kid is going to come after me. I say,

- Damn it, why can't life be simple?

The bartender gives me a look to settle down. Without looking up from his cards, one of the old guys says,

- 'Cause once you beat it, then what?

The other guy he's playing cards with says,

- Drink and play cards. That's what.

They cheers their drinks and chuckle.

They go back to playing cards. I go back to drinking and thinking. What do I do with the body? Chopping it up could be an option. A power tool is necessary for that. I have a hand saw that runs on elbow grease. Chopping it would be filled with blood and guts, though. I don't think I could handle that. I'm not a monster. I cough out some of my beer at the thought of this. The bartender glares at me. I wave her off and grab a napkin.

Maybe I should ask Jon. He's probably isn't doing anything. His phone goes to voicemail. I leave a message,

  – Hey Jon, how be Cleveland so far? I wish I
  could say that it's been the same old shit here
  but I can't. Call me back.

I toss the phone on the bar and order another beer. The bartender studies me as she brings me the beer. I want to tell her to take a chill pill. This is only my second beer. Instead, a smile and a thank you is what she gets. While taking a sip of my beer, Jon texts me. It's a picture of a girl doing a pin-up girl pose in her underwear. The text reads

  : Cleveland Rocks!!!
  I write back,
  : I'll be damned. Drew Carey was right.
  : She lives in Vegas.
  : Boo.
  : Cleveland is okay. It will get better after I
  adjust.
  : If you had to dispose of a body, how would
  you?
  : What kind of question is that?
  : Ahh, I'm at a bar, and the winner gets a free
  beer.
  : Simplest might be the best. Bury it in the
  woods.
  : Don't you think someone would find it?
  : Body would decompose by the time it's found.
  : You think?
  : Bugs need to eat. Dip it in honey then bury it.
  Final answer.
  : Weirdo.

: Who did you kill?

A voice I recognize pulls me away from my phone. Monica, in all of her glory and as lovely as ever, sits beside me. Her hair is shiny, and her aura matches. She says,

- Is this seat taken?
- Of all the empty seats, you have to sit on this one.

She immediately gets up. I grab her arm and say,

- Just joking.

She sits. With a smirk, she says,

- What happened to the sunshine?
- Is it dark already?
- No dingy, your fortune that you will bring sunshine into someone's life.
- Oh. Let me tell you about that.

The bartender comes over before we call her. She says,

- Hey, Monica, rum and coke?

Monica answers as she gets situated,

- You know it. How are you?
- Same old, same old.
- That's why I love this place.

The bartender brings over her drink and says,

- Watch out for this one. He drinks.

I say,

- What's that supposed to mean?

The bartender raises her eyes to Monica. Monica answers,

- I already know he's crazy. Aren't we all sometimes.

No one, let alone a girl, admits that they're crazy. I say,

- I thought you said your days were dull.
- Dull mostly, but that doesn't mean I'm not

crazy. Doesn't everyone let loose sometimes?
I'm not saying I would kill someone. But if it
came down to it, I hope I could if I had to.
Judging by what I know of you, surely you
could kill someone if you had to.

I feel my head turning bright red. There is nothing I can do to
stop it. I say,

    – Where is this coming from? Why would you
    say that?

    – Whoa there, cowboy. Not sure why you're
    getting all defensive. I'm just breaking the ice.

Monica gets up and moves down a stool. The bartender looks
over with concern. I move beside Monica. My hand extends to
her. I say,

    – Hi, sunshine. What are you doing here during
    the day?

    – Every Wednesday I have a drink to celebrate
    hump day. I could ask you the same question,
    sunshine.

    – Well, it just so happens that I a little birdie told
    me you might be here so I figured that I'd come
    and say hello. Maybe create a little sunshine.

    – Which birdie is that? I got a bone to pick with
    him. Was it the brown one?

    – It was the black one.

    – Why's it always got to be the black one?

    – Ahh. I didn't mean anything by it.

    – Got ya.

I slam the rest of my beer. Even though Monica said it was a
joke, it works me up. I say,

    – I probably deserve that.

- You are one strange cat, Eddie.
- Naw, you just caught me in a transition period.
- Is that it, is it?
- Some might say that people do crazy things
when they don't have a set path.
- No life coaching, please.

My eyes dart up as an eerie feeling runs through me like that of a graveyard walk during a full moon. Entering the bar is the other rapist. He has a scowl on his face. He's probably pissed that his friend is missing. My head immediately turns to Monica. The thought that he's going to kill me is the only thing going through my head. I kiss Monica to hide my face. Her lips aren't receptive. After the initial shock wears off, her soft full lips kiss me back. She tries to break from my embrace. I pull her into a hug. She resists in a polite way. I hold her in my arms and say,

- This may sound weird but could you help me
with something? Whisper your answer.
- I'll help.
- The guy who just walked in wants to beat my
ass for some reason. Ever since we were in jail,
he and his friend have been after me.
- You were in jail?
- Just for questioning, to scare me. The guy
that walked in is the reason I was hiding at the
coffee shop. I'll tell you all about it later.
- What do you need from me?
- A distraction so I can get out of here. And his
name.

The rapist is sitting on a stool between us and the door. He's waiting for his drink. My eyes watch him carefully. He seems angrier than usual. I wait for my moment to get past him. My head buries in Monica's neck every time he looks over. She smells like a flower bed on a spring afternoon. Just as the bartender gives him his drink, Monica shoves me off of her and yells,

– Who the fuck do you think you are? You think
you can just come up to me and kiss me after
being with that bitch.

My back is facing the door. Monica is facing the rapist. I'm taken completely off guard by her action.

– Monica, please. I didn't do anything, I swear.

– Oh, and I'm supposed to believe that. I can
smell that bitch on you. And then you come in
here and try to kiss me. Fuck you.

She pushes me toward the door. I don't like it, but it makes sense.

– Please, I didn't do anything. I swear. It's only
you baby. You're the only one for me. You
know that.

Everyone in the bar watches us. The two old guys look up from their card game possibly for the second time all day. The bartender yells,

– I knew you trouble. Out!

Monica throws her drink in my face as we near the rapist. My hands cover my face as I wipe the rum and coke from my eyes. As I do, a foot hits me square in the nuts. All the air leaves my body, I say,

– Mother fucker. You...

– And don't you ever come into the coffee shop
in the morning when I'm there at 10. You dick!

The whole bar cheers. I curl over in pain. Monica spins me around and kicks me out the door. My body hits the cold ground.

The bar door slams shut. The people inside cheer. I roll on the ground in pain. That is not what I was expecting. I wipe my watery eyes, dust myself off, and get the hell out of there.

At home, instead of thinking about what to do about the body, I reflect on the softness of Monica's lips. They felt like fluffy pillows of love. It was like nothing existed but our lips. It didn't feel that way when it was happening, but that's how I remember it now. Not sure if I should write this but masturbation to black women porn is what I do next. The thought of Monica keeps me company.

Today is the least lonely I've felt in some time. Thanks, Monica. Maybe we could fall in love.

# 24

## Day 24

The morning sun wakes me as it shines through the window. Its glow covers me with light and freshness to start the day. It makes me think that Nelson Mandela was right when he talked about letting your light shine. I'm going to look up his quote after I do some push-ups and sit-ups. I do three sets of 25 each. Then do one extra set of each because I feel so good. Here's the Nelson Mandela quote from his inaugural speech:

"Our deepest fear is not that we are inadequate. Our deepest fear is that we are powerful beyond measure. It is our light, not our darkness that most frightens us. We ask ourselves. Who am I to be brilliant, gorgeous, talented, fabulous? Actually, who are you not to be? You are a child of God. Your playing small does not serve the world. There is nothing enlightened about shrinking so that other people won't feel insecure around you. We are all meant to shine, as children do. We were born to make manifest the glory of God that is within us. It's not just in some of us; it's in everyone. And as we let our own light shine, we unconsciously give other people permission to do the same. As we are liberated from our own fear, our presence automatically

liberates others."
  - Nelson Mandela

This quote will be my copilot. It will go with me everywhere. First stop is the shower. The falling water cleanses me of yesterday's news and reminds me that today is fantastic and so am I. My light needs to shine. When it shines, I shine. Maybe I don't need Nora to shine my light. The recent happenings have been a bit of a pill to swallow, but it feels as if my light has returned. It seems as if hope has returned. Maybe Monica can be my light. Maybe the guy in the garage is my catalyst for change like I was the catalyst for change for Nora. This is the best shower ever.

Coffee is in order. Or should I say, Monica is in order? Her instructions were easy to figure out even after a kick to the nuts. Hopefully, the mean kid wasn't paying attention to the subtext. Certainly, the show would have kept his attention.

I park down the street from the coffee shop then read the Mandela quote again. It inspires me to do my energy exercises. My routine gets my energy flowing like a raging river after a monsoon. My hands feel like they are holding balls of energy. I actively move my energy around my body. It makes me tingle all over. I feel electric.

It feels like I'm floating down the street. Everyone seems to be interested in me. People say hi as they pass. One guy in his twenties nods to me from across the street. I nod back. A young artsy-hipster girl, the type that usually doesn't give me the time of day, smirks as she passes. Finally, the girls I'm attracted to are giving me some attention. I stop to contemplate my next move. Should I talk to the hipster girl? I keep walking. Monica is my light's obsession today.

Monica is sitting at an outside table reading a magazine. It's hard to tell which magazine because she folds the pages around the back. My guess would be US or Cosmo. She is sipping a large coffee. She looks very metro-hip. She has a scarf on and big round sunglasses that cover most of her beautiful face. The collar of her jacket is raised up. She almost looks like she is trying to hide out. It makes me think of a spy movie. For fun, I attempt to sneak past her to get a coffee before greeting her. I hear a whispering voice say,

– I see you.

I turn, and Monica raises her sunglasses and smiles at me. I say,

– I'm going to get a coffee.

She lowers her glasses and goes back to reading. It's almost as if this is a spy movie. I'm not sure which of us is the spy. While waiting in the three person line, all I can think about is how cute Monica looks today. Was she always that pretty? I don't know, but I like it. I think of the Mandela quote while waiting my turn. "We are all meant to shine as children do." My energy flows through me. It reminds me of its presence. My glow returns. The cute barista girl takes my order of a large coffee with no room. The smile and eye batting she gives me are enough to stop any man in his tracks. My typical reaction would be to blush. Today, I say,

– Thank you. Did anyone ever tell you that you
have a beautiful glow? Hold on to that. It's
special.

Her eyes look down then back at me. If looks could kill, she just killed me with beauty. I smile and say,

– Stay Golden.

I chuckle as I walk back to Monica. It's less of a chuckle and more of a smile of fulfillment. I grab a newspaper off another table. I open the paper to block my face and sit. It's like we are two spies talking. She notices what I'm doing and does the same with her magazine. Through her magazine, she says,
- Why are we doing this?
- Doesn't it feel like we're in a spy movie?
- It feels like a coffee shop.
She lowers her magazine. I say,
- Not yet.
She quickly puts it back up again and says,
- What? I want to see your face.
My eyes peer over the top of the paper. They dart around making sure the coast is clear. Monica pulls down the paper and says,
- Are you done Inspector Gadget?
- You're the one that dressed like a sexy super spy. I'm just following suit.
- Why? The scarf?
- Everything. The mystery. The allure. You scream superstar. Super spy.
Her eyes look at me like I must be joking. I pull the paper back up in front of my face. She pulls it down. I leave it down and take in her beauty. There is a moment of silence as we both take in each other. Just as I'm about to say something, Monica does,
- Before you say anything, I just want to say that yesterday was quite an experience for me. I'm not saying I liked it, maybe the acting part of kicking you, but the rest, I'm not so sure.
- I'm sorry you had to be a part of that. I'll try to keep you from it from now on.

- What do you mean from now on?
- I thought we could see what happens. Is that presumptuous?

She pulls her magazine up to her face and says,
- I liked it. All of it.

I pull the newspaper up to my face and say,
- Really?
- It was the most fun I had in weeks. Months even. Except for you in the coffee shop the other day.

I lower the paper and say,
- Really?

She pulls the paper back up and says,
- Yeah.

The look in her eyes is absolute intrigue. Her eyes are full of excitement and possibly lust. Her reaction is not what I was expecting. We both lower our face guards. I sip my coffee. She grabs my hand and says,
- You're the person I've been looking for. I want in your world. May I come in?
- You sound like a vampire trying to get in a house.
- Seriously?
- Seriously, I would like nothing more.

She squeezes my hand then grabs my face and kisses me on the lips. It's not a huge kiss, but I feel it. It feels glorious through my whole body. Her pillow lips leave me with a smile. Her voice takes me out of my wonder-lust when she says,
- Don't you want to know what happened?
- Yeah. Sorry. I'm caught up in this real-life moment.

Our eyes take in each other's beauty. It feels as if energy is buzzing all around us. It's as if we are meant to be. Smiles fill our faces. She mimics like she's taking a bite out of me. She squeezes my hand and says,

- After you left, the kid sits beside me. He buys
me a drink to replace the one I threw on you.
He says "a pertty darling like you don't deserve
that shit. Why don't you drop the zero and get
with the hero."
- He quoted a Vanilla Ice movie.
- That's from a movie?
- Keep going.
- Then he says, "darlin', I'll make you scream."
I say "excuse me?" He says "you're better than
that life coach fucker. I'm the fucking man in
this town. What I say goes. And I say you
should be with me. How you like them apples?"
I can't believe my ears. Monica sips her coffee. I say,
- Life coach fucker? What an asshole.
- Yeah. And he puts his hand on my leg and says
"You like that don't you?" I grab his dick and
squeezes as hard as I can and say "you like that
you fucking prick?!" His face begins turning
red. At this point the bartender notices. She
comes over and takes the remainder of his drink
and says "Time to go." I say "no no, I'll go."
As I get up, he grabs my arm. I throw the drink
he bought me in his face and say "talk to me
again, and it'll be the end." Then I storm out of
there.
- You're fucking crazier than he is. He has been

after me, and now you antagonize him.

– He doesn't know we're together.

– We're together?

– You know what I mean.

– "Talk to me again, and it'll be the end." That sounds like a movie line. Where did you get that?

– One of my old boyfriends would say that when he wanted me to shut up.

– Did it work?

– No.

– I wouldn't think so.

I grab her hands and take in her beauty. Her pillow lips purse. Her eyes flinch with excitement. She says,

– So, can we hang out or what?

– It would be my honor to be with you, Monica.

She squeezes my hands. I lean toward her. Our lips touch. This time, there is a little tongue involved. It feels better than imagined. The waitress bumps my chair as she passes. I don't want to stop but can take a hint. When we break from our kiss, the look in her eyes is perfection. Surely, the look in mine is the same. No words are necessary. Our kiss says it all. She coyly takes a drink of her coffee. I do the same. It takes a minute to get off of cloud 9. She says,

– Oh shit.

– What?

– I'm late for work.

– Can you call in?

– What kind of life coach are you?

– It's called work, not life.

– Honey, sometimes you got to work to get the life.

\- How about after?

\- Call me.

She hands me her card. Then gives me a kiss. I try to hold on to her. She breaks free and says,

\- I get off at 5 p.m.

\- Have a good day.

\- You too.

She waves and scurries away. Her wave and smile give me a fuzzy feeling. Her business card is on thick stock paper. Even it feels good to the touch. I lean back and sip my coffee with a smile. Nelson Mandela rules.

While sitting in my car figuring out how to spend the rest of this splendid day, a good song comes on the radio, which is a rarity. It is the perfect song for today. It's Modern English's song: "I Melt With You." I scream along to the music. My phone begins to buzz. It's Officer Dave. I know because I put his number in my phone, so I'll always know it's him.

\- This is Eddie.

I now know what I'm doing today. Officer Dave wants me to come down to the station. He says he has a matter to discuss. If I prefer, he can send some units to pick me up. Driving myself sounds like a better option.

They put me in the same interrogation room and leave me there. I sit there for at least twenty minutes before Officer Dave enters. I say,

\- I feel like I'm under arrest.

\- Why? Did you do something that we don't know about?

\- I don't think so.

- That's a strange answer. You don't remember?
- Trust me. I'd remember. We're cool. What did you want to talk about?
- It seems that we have had another complaint from a Miss Eva Collins. She is stating that you came over to her house again.
- She called and asked me to. I swear. I didn't want to go, but she begged. So, I did. She seemed unstable, but not suicidal, so I left. That's it. I knocked on the door. I swear.
- She is claiming that you went over to her house and got her all worked up then you left her there in an agitated state which is dangerous for someone in her condition.
- That may be true, but she invited me under the pretense that she was suicidal. It's my job to check on my patients.
- Do you still have patients if you closed your practice?
- Umm, I didn't close it forever.
- But it is closed?
- Yes.
- So technically she is no longer your patient.
- Technically, but.
- There are no buts, except yours in jail. Is that what you want?
- Absolutely not.
- Is a restraining order necessary?
- I don't think she'll come after me.
- For her.
- That won't be necessary. I'll call her today and

let her know that my practice is currently shut
down and that she'll have to find a new doctor.
 - And that is all you're going to say. Nothing
more.
 - Yes, sir.
 - Get out of here. I don't want to see you again.
I get up to leave and wipe my forehead dry at the same time. I
don't think Officer Dave noticed. He says,
 - One more thing. Do you know a David
Undercuffler?
 - I don't know who that is.
 - I ask because you were in our holding cell at
the same time. He always hangs around another
kid. They're troublemakers. Did you hear
anything?
My forehead begins dripping sweat again. I wipe it without
thinking. He says,
 - Why are you sweating?
 - Jail sucked and I don't want to go back. He
and his friend terrorized me in there.
 - It didn't look like it.
 - You opened the cell just as I was about to be
beaten down by them. All I said to them was
that they should Stay Golden and maybe they
wouldn't be in there.
 - Have you seen him since?
 - No, sir. Wait, yes. I'll saw the two of them
driving.
 - When was that?
 - A couple of days ago. I was going to the coffee
shop. I tried to cover my face so they wouldn't

see me.
- Did they?
- They gave me the finger.
- That's it?
- I ran. I didn't want any trouble.
- That's it?
- That's it, sir.
- That will be all. Stay away from Eva Collins,
or you're going back to jail.
- Sir, she's not my patient anymore.

I get to my car and make a phone call. It rings and rings. It goes to voicemail. I leave a message,
- Hey, Monica, it's Eddie. How about after work
you come to my place? I'll cook you dinner. Let
me know so I can prepare. Have a beautiful day
sunshine.
That sounded pretty good. Hopefully, Monica gets back to me soon. I set the phone on the dash and put on my seatbelt. Almost instantly, my phone buzzes. I answer without looking.
- Hey, sweet 'ems.
- Hey, Eddie. I like that, sweet 'ems.
I look at the phone, and it's Eva. Her ears must have been ringing.
- Sorry, I thought this was someone else. What
can I do for you, Eva?
- I don't feel so well. Can you come over?
- Eva, I can't. I had to shut down my practice, so
you'll have to find a new life coach or doctor.
- What if I don't want another doctor?
- I'm sorry, Eva. I can no longer advise you.

– Please, Eddie, I need you. Please, don't leave me. Please.

– I'm sorry. I have to go. Have a good day.

I hang up. That was easier than expected. A text came in while I was talking. It's Monica. She says that dinner sounds perfect and that she gets off at 5 p.m.

Shopping and cleaning are in order. After that, I have a drink. I suppose that tonight could be just a date with a new girl. To me, it's a new beginning. It's a chance to open myself up and let Golden Love in and my Golden Love out. That sounds yummy in my tummy. This tequila shot tastes perfect. Another shot is in order.

While sitting on the couch enjoying a glass of wine and a relaxed feeling, there's a knock at the door. A buzz of energy flows through me. It's time to shine. I attempt to push the wrinkles out of my sweater then answer the door. Regret fills me as I open the door. Why didn't I look first?

– Hi, Eddie.

– What are you doing here, Eva?

– I had to come. I need you.

– It's a bad time. And as I said before Eva, I have closed my practice.

– Can I come in? It's chilly out here.

– I'm sorry, but I'm expecting company any minute now.

– How about just until they get here? Then I'll leave.

She looks at me with her big brown puppy dog eyes.

– Fine. But for just a minute.

– You're so kind.

She pushes the door closed and herself closer to me. Her slender body and round breasts push up against my body. It turns me on a little. I step back. She follows. She keeps her body tight against mine and says,

– You're the only doctor for me.

Her hand strokes my face then down my chest. She unbuttons her coat, slides it to the floor, and presses her see-through lingerie covered body against mine and moans. Her arms begin rubbing up and down my back. She wraps her leg around mine and locks herself against me. She says,

– I don't care what name you call me. I just need
your love. You complete me.

She tries to grab my face to kiss me. I do my best to resist. She lands a few kisses. Her body rubbing against mine makes my little friend rise to the occasion. My hands grab her and hold her away from me. She moans again. It's as if she likes it rough.

– Enough. I am not your doctor. You are not my
patient. That means that we have nothing more
to say to one another.

She stands there quietly and looks up at me. The hurt behind her eyes is on full display. I firm my stance and say,

– Eva, listen to me. This thing you think we
have, it doesn't exist. I do love you, but not the
way you think. Now, I believe that what you're
trying to do is healthy and is a positive step for
you. It's just not healthy to blindly do it.

– Blindly follow your heart? Isn't that Staying
Golden?

– It is. But you can't just blindly do it.

She practically throws herself at me and says,

– I love you. Why can't you love me? Love me.

Please, love me.

There's a knock on the door.

– Stop this. Now.

– But, I love you.

– My company is here. You need to get it
together and go.

I cover her with her coat. There's another knock on the door,
this time louder.

– Please don't ruin this for me.

– But, I love you.

I push her toward the door and open it. Standing in the
doorway and looking like an angel from heaven is Monica. Her
smile quickly turns to a frown when she sees a barely dressed
woman being pushed out. I say,

– Hey, Monica. This is Eva. She's an old patient
of mine who needed some assistance.

Eva gives me a kiss on the cheek. With a huge smile, she says,

– You're the best doctor ever.

– Eva, I closed my practice.

As Eva walks away, she says,

– For now.

Monica looks at me funny. Before she can say anything, I say,

– That is not what you think.

Monica says,

– She's an infatuated patient who sees you as a
door to her feelings and can't separate you as
just her doctor.

– Okay. Maybe it is what it seems. Can we start
over?

– Sure.

I close the door with Monica still outside. My hands fix my

shirt and my hair. I jump up and down to get loose. Monica knocks on the door. I shake my limbs out to get my energy flowing. I open the door.

- Hi.
- Hey, Monica. Come in, come in.

I give her a hug and a kiss on the cheek. She hands me her jacket and a bottle of wine. The jacket lands on a chair as we walk toward the kitchen with the wine. I say,

- You okay with all of this?
- Eddie, this is exactly what I want. I'm
intrigued.

I pull her in and lay a big kiss on her. I push her away and walk into the kitchen. There's a smirk on my face that she doesn't see. She says,

- Well, hello to you too.
- I hope you like cheese. I'm figuring we have
some cheese, salami, and some veggies. Then
follow it up with either ice cream or steak.

I have a spread already made up with all the fixings. There's cheese, crackers, olive bread, broccoli, two kinds of salami, and some humus. Monica's eyes widen at the sight. I pop a bottle of champagne, and the festivities begin. We don't last very long, only an hour-and-a-half or so before we find ourselves in the bedroom. Without giving away all the details, I'll just say that I gave her my Golden Love, and she was open to receive it.

# 25

## Day 25

I wake to the gray light of a cloud covered sky. I roll over to cuddle Monica, and she's gone. Where she was laying is now cold. She must have left early. My phone reads 1030 a.m. I roll over and snuggle the pillow that she used. Her sweet smell remains. A cozy feeling fills me with delight. My body buzzes with goodness. It's like all of the neutrons have left my body and all that remains are protons. And they're jubilant about it. Monica sends me a text. It's like she knew I was thinking of her. It reads,

: Had SO MUCH FUN last night! Had to run.

Nice motorcycle. I'll text you later. Have a great

day. P.S. I think something died in your garage.

- Oh, Shit!

I practically fall out of bed. The floor is cold. It sends a chill through my body. It makes my walk brisk. That and the thought that I could be found out.

The garage smells of death. My hand covers my mouth and nose in hopes to block the smell. I survey the area. Everything seems to be in order. The bike is still in the same place. More importantly, the trash can still has the lid on it. And the box I put on top of it is still there. Maybe she didn't see anything.

I go outside to give my nose a break. My nostrils may be scarred for life. Only a little bit of the death smell gets out into the open air. It should get eaten up by the many trees lining the streets.

My cold feet hurry me back to bed. I lie there like a little sick child with the covers pulled up to my chin. I think to myself. This is some crazy shit. Or am I a guy doing what needs to be done, righting a wrong.

The first stop on this crazy train of a day is the grocery store. It's every grocery store in town. At the first store, I buy six twelve-ounce honey bears. More would have been in order, but that's all they have.

At the second store, I buy five more. The cashier looks at me funny. I say,

– What can I say? I'm feeling sweet.

A smile fuels my exit. Why don't stores sell honey in bulk like they do sugar?

The third store only has four. It's weird that there isn't more honey considering all the bees in the summer. The cashier looks at me funny. This time, I say,

– Sweet is as sweet does.

Again, my exit is fueled by a smile. It feels like I know something everyone else doesn't. And it's a good thing. I high-tail it to my place to get the final piece of the puzzle. I cover my face like a bandit from the old west and enter. It helps. The first thing I need is a tarp to roll the body in. Thank you, gangster movies for giving me insight. A sleeping bag will have to do. I unzip it and lay it on the floor. Fear fills me as I'm about to open the lid. What will be under there, bugs, shit, a blue human? I chicken out.

Two shots of tequila help prepare me for the task at hand. One more is in order. Now the time feels right. I put the bandana over my face and march into the garage with the purpose of a bandit. A feeling of power runs through me as I stand over the trash can.

– That's right. I killed you because you're a
fucking dick. Wait, you WERE a dick. Now
you're right where you belong!

My hand lifts the lid. A now blue head stares at me. His eyes are open. I jump back.

– Fucking asshole!

I find some work gloves before I touch this stinky thing. I close the dead eyes. The smell is beginning to get to me. I yank the bandana down and let the puke fly. I was aiming for the sleeping bag but overshot it by a foot or two. I kick the trash can in disgust. It doesn't budge. It doesn't even wobble. With all of my might, I tackle the can forward landing right on top of the sleeping bag and right beside the pile of puke. I try to pull the can off of the body. That doesn't work either. There's one option left, and it's the least likable. I'll pull the body out. For a dead guy, he sure has resiliency. It's as if the body wants to stay in the trash can. That is where it belongs. But then how would I get it into the woods? How would I cover it with honey so that the animals will eat it?

The rape pops into my head. How could they do that to someone? Anger floods my veins like a dose of hard drugs. It gives me the gusto to do this thing. It's not an easy task. He's a stiff alright. And he managed to wedge himself in there. I grab him by the head and pull. I use my feet to push the can. His body pops out, and his head almost face-plants on my nuts. If I were one to believe in luck, this would be one of those moments. A kick in his dead ass is my reward for a job well done. I zip the sleeping bag and tape the top closed. I puke in my mouth twice in the process. When I finish the wrap job, a few more kicks are in order.

The drive to the woods consists of the windows down and the floor heat blasting. I troll along at exactly two miles-per-hour over the limit. Def Leppard is my co-pilot on this journey. "Rock of Ages" comes on. I crank it up and sing along.

My usual parking spot outside the woods is waiting for me. The first thing I do is get out and inhale some clean air. The dead smell made the car feel like a dungeon.

The woods' air rejuvenates me like it would a plant. I take a moment and imagine myself as a tree connected to the forest. It helps me focus on the task at hand. My limbs begin to feel more limber. Jumping around completes my process. I'm ready. My eyes survey the area. There doesn't seem to be anyone around.

I grab the honey and set it beside the trunk of my Corolla. As the trunk opens, the fumes of death almost knock me on the ground. I begin coughing aggressively. A car slows as it passes. The guy driving puts his window down and asks,

– Is everything okay?

– I'm good. Just a little woozy.

– You want me to call someone? You look kinda sick.

– I got it. Thanks for stopping.

– Suit yourself.

– Good day.

The good Samaritan raises my paranoid level up to eleven. My heart is beating so fast that any physical exertion could give me a heart attack. If only someone were here to help. Crime might be better if you have someone to share it with. Jon picked a fine time to move back to Ohio.

   – Life coach to fucking murderer, Jesus Fucking
Christ, what have I become?


The woods seem lifeless. They're usually filled with sounds of animals and blowing brush. Today, they're quiet and eerie. The body is heavy, and so is the smell. I stop three times before getting to the ridge above the body's final resting place.

At the ridge, the body drops on the ground and so do I. A well-deserved rest is in order. Getting this all done at an accelerated pace was the plan. I didn't take into account the weight or the smell. When my nerves calm, which I don't know if they will, it's time to finish this thing.

Nora pops into my head while I unwrap the body. She pops in like she used to when we were connected. Nora is so beautiful and full of love. I take a moment to remember. She's the one who reminds me what emotions are. A smile fills my face.

   – Oh, sweet Nora, how I love thee.

A moment of silence follows.

I become a busy bee spreading its honey. I focus on covering the head first. It takes two full honey bears to cover his head. One of his eyes open and sends me into the air. I land on my ass and a rock. It hurts. I may as well break while I'm sitting. My wrists are tired from all the squeezing. Nora's sweetness pops into my head again. She may be the only thing in the world sweeter than honey.

It takes ten honey bears to cover the front. My foot and a

branch manage to roll the body over. It smells like shit. I get to squeezing while singing "Pour Some Sugar on Me" by Def Leppard,

I use two branches to roll the honey-covered body to the edge. There's so much dirt and debris already covering the body that it's barely recognizable. With a final goodbye push, I say,

– Die, die my darling.

And there he goes. His body rolls down the hill bumping trees and rocks leaving his scent everywhere for animals to smell. As the body rolls, it appears to be gaining size. It's beginning to look like a dirt wrapped mummy.

– I hope the bears don't mind.

My face hides in my hands at the thought of the dirt covering up the honey smell. After a moment of hoping for the best, I hear,

– What are you doing?

I look up. It's Monica. She's standing over the sleeping bag full of empty honey bears and staring at me. I say,

– What are you doing?

– I saw the whole thing.

– Why are you here? Are you following me? Tell me. Are you fucking following me? What are you a fucking cop or something?

– Would a cop sleep with you last night?

– I don't see why not. Answer the question.

Monica doesn't say anything. She just looks at me and the area. I say,

– It's not that hard. Are you a cop and are you following me? Answer me, Monica.

– What did you just dropped down there?

– Answer the fucking question, Monica, before

things get fucking crazy. Answer!
- I'm not a cop, Eddie. I swear.
- Why are you fucking following me?
- I don't know, Eddie...
Tears of fear begin to fill her eyes. She continues,
- You know I've been looking for adventure.
When I saw your motorcycle, I love bikes and
couldn't resist looking at it. The door was
unlocked. It smelled awful, so I tried to see
what it was. I was going to take it to the trash.
Then I saw it. Oh, it was so much worse than I
thought.
My eyes stay glued to Monica. She hides her tear filled face in
her hands. When she raises her head back up, an almost sinister
look is in her eyes. She says,
- I kinda liked it. The thought of me and a dead
body in the same building is exactly the
excitement that I've been looking for. Eddie,
you're exactly what I've been looking for.
Adventure. Living above the line. Good in bed.
- Hold on a second. You saw a dead body and
liked it?
- Yes.
- You know I'm a life coach, and that's not okay.
- When you killed him, did you like it?
- You think I'm good in bed?
Monica cocks her head and glares at me to answer the question.
My stance shifts to a nervous shuffle.
- Maybe.
- Yes or no?
- I'm the one asking the questions. I can't believe

you were following me. Maybe I can. But it
doesn't make it alright. We have to be able to
trust each other. Can I trust you?

Her eyes turn cutesy. She looks up and says,

– You can trust me. Can I trust you?

I take a moment to think. Monica saw the body and liked it.
She now knows where it is. I say,

– We're in this together now.

She smirks and rushes up beside me to see the body at the
bottom. She says,

– Where is it? Is that it?

– The raised clump of ground right there.

– That's it? Good job.

– Hope so.

Monica kisses me. Not one of those little kisses either. It's
more of a traffic stopping and people cheering kind of kiss. It's
the kind where the girl kicks her foot back, and the story is
happily over. In this case, it's just beginning. I say,

– What was that for?

– For being you. For being perfect.

– We should go.

We pack up the honey bears in the sleeping bag and get
moving. I stop us at the spot where the alleged rape happened.
She says,

– Why are we stopping?

– I want to do something.

– What's so special about this place?

I begin breathing exercises hoping to align myself with the
flowing energy of the world. Monica sits on a rock and watches.
She is my first audience. It slows the process. As my connection
begins to build, flashes of the rape begin to appear in my head.

I grab Monica's hands and say,

– Don't say anything. Just close your eyes and
feel.

Her hands squeeze mine tight. My focus stays on the flashes
of the rape. When it becomes too much to bear, I throw down
her hand and sit on the downed tree that's beside me. Monica is
frozen and wide-eyed like a deer in headlights. She sits across
from me on a moss covered rock. We don't speak. A cold wind
blows through. I feel a cold chill on my neck. Monica must feel
it too because she moves beside me and grabs my hand. I say,

– Could you see it?

– I felt it. Whatever it was.

– The guy at the bottom of the ridge, he and his
friend, raped a girl. I saw some of it then fell
and knocked myself out.

– Can we talk about this at your place?


She holds my hand for dear life. It's probably for safety. I
hope it's for something more. She says,

– Where did you learn to do that?

– Get rid of a body? I asked my friend.

– No. Pass images.

– I call it passing energy. It's my superpower.
Everyone has one thing they can do better than
anyone. A.k.a superpower.

She looks at me with a smile of understanding and perhaps
contentment. It makes me feel super. We get out of the woods.
She is parked right behind me. The coast looks clear. I say,

– I'll see you at my place.

She gives me a full-on kiss on the mouth. We probably
shouldn't be kissing, but her lips feel too good to stop. Our

kisses always seem to be magical. I say,

   – We need to go.

   Back at my place, we take the metal trash can that the body was in and fill it with yesterday's newspapers. Then the sleeping bag and the honey bears fill the can to the top. Lighter fluid and some matches are the icings on the cake. I say,

   – Burn, baby burn. Burning it is a good idea.

   – Duh, don't you watch TV?

   – That shit poisons the brain.

Monica rubs my back and says,

   – It's a good thing I'm here.

Monica radiates as the fire's light glistens off her face. It makes her look majestic like a queen, and if she's the queen, then I'm the king. We watch as evil tyranny burns away. She kisses my cheek and grabs my hand. I give her hand a squeeze. It feels good to be with someone.

# 26

## Day 26

The TV is blasting today's news while I make coffee. Monica enters wearing one of my dress shirts. He skinny-yet-toned legs hold her up with sheer beauty. She is the perfect thing for my eyes to gaze upon this lovely morning. The very sight of her beautiful brown eyes launches me to the moon. She kisses me with her pillow lips and grabs a coffee. She plants her perfectly round butt on the couch beside me and sips her drink.

A smile fills my face. It feels like everything was supposed to happen to lead up to this point. It's funny. One would think that killing someone would be a curse. To me, it seems to be more of a blessing. I don't believe in God, but if I did, I would thank him for this moment.

I can't seem to get enough of Monica or her lips. Her eyes tell me that she feels the same. We don't say much. We don't have to as long as our bodies are touching. She moves closer to me which is next to impossible considering we are already touching. I like it and say,

- What time do you work today?
- Fridays, I work half days. 12 p.m. to 5 p.m.
- Thank God. We got some time.

– I didn't know you believed in God.

I adjust myself. Talking about God is always a challenge. I continue,

– I believe he is the inner light that shines in all
of us.

– Does that count?

I say,

– To me, it's just an expression like "holy cow."
Or "how about them apples?"

– I like "how about them apples?" If God is real,
I want to thank him for you.

A playful smirk fills me. I say,

– For me or "how about them apples?"

She kisses me.

On the TV, the news is talking about a missing kid. We listen intently. Monica asks,

– Is that him?

– Yep.

– His name is David Undercuffler?

– That's what the cop said his name was.

– The cops know?

She pushes herself off of me. Her demeanor changes to worry. She asks,

– What do the police know?

– Nothing. They know that we were in jail for a
few hours together. That's it.

– Are you sure?

– Yeah, I think so. They were talking to me
about being a peeping Tom.

– You're a peeping Tom too?

– Not exactly.

- I forgive and like adventure, but some
things aren't acceptable even in my book.
- You have a book? Is that like a stalker
handbook?
- Are you calling me a stalker?
- I was kidding. One of my patients left me a
message that she was feeling suicidal, so I went
to her house. She happened to be coming out of
the shower as I was looking in the window to
see if she was okay. That's it. She was in an
agitated state and called the cops. It was all just
a misunderstanding. I may have killed someone,
but I am not a pervert.
- Good 'cause that don't fly in my book.
- Mine neither.
- You have a book?
I kiss her. She pushes me off. We go back to watching the
news. Patrick Doyle is on TV talking about the missing kid.
Patrick is the other bully. Monica says,
- There's the asshole from the bar.
We watch the TV carefully.
- "I'm so worried about my friend Dave. We
have been friends since we were seven. He has
never done anything like this. He would have
told me. We're like brothers. He is one of those
guys who is a light to the community, and as
long as he is missing, the community will
suffer. Please, if anyone knows of his
whereabouts, please, please, please come
forward."
Patrick wipes his eyes like he is crying. I say,

- What a crock of shit.
- That guy should get an acting award for that.
- Hopefully, bears will eat the body.
- Was that your plan, the bears eat the body?
- They like honey, don't they?
- I know what you're doing when I go to work.
- What?
- Speaking of, I have to go.
- A quickie?

She looks at the time. Then grabs my hand and leads me into the bedroom.

Today is warm. The sun feels good as it shines on me. The woods smell alive. They feel very inviting, unlike yesterday. As I get deeper in, the leaf filled branches blanket the forest giving it a cold chill. Usually, this would feel good, but today it feels eerie. Maybe it's all in my head. The shadows of the branches make it feel as if someone is following me. Every few steps, I make sure that isn't the case. There is no one around, but I would swear there is.

The sun hides behind the clouds as I approach the rape spot. Goosebumps rise on my arms. My steps quicken. A loose rock makes me fall to the ground. Blood begins to flow from my left palm. The blood flashes me back to the rape. This time images don't pop into my head. This time it is the sound of her screaming. It's haunting. I suck the blood from my hand and scurry out of there as fast as I can.

I get to the hilltop where the honey covering took place and peer over the edge. While looking over the edge, a gust of wind pushes up from the valley and smacks me in the face. I'm not talking about a gentle breeze either. I'm talking about a full-on gust of wind leftover from a tornado. If I were wearing a hat, it would be in the next county.

I begin summoning up my positive energy with breathing exercises. Usually, I can feel my heat in seconds. This time it takes minutes. As my body starts to buzz, I attempt to look over the edge. Another wind gust, bringing dirt with it, smacks me in the face. I shield myself with my arm and manage to see the body. It appears that it hasn't been anything's dinner yet. It looks the same as it did.

– Damn it, Jon. Why did I listen to you?

– Who's Jon?

I jump. Whoever is behind me scares the shit out of me. I turn. It's Tammy. I say,

– What the hell are you doing here?

– Same as you, I suppose.

– What's that?

– Hiking.

– Yeah, it's a good day for it.

A wave of relief calms me a bit. Just a bit because you can never be too sure about Tammy. I move away from the edge in hopes that she won't look. She says,

– Who's Jon?

– He's my friend that moved to Cleveland. He told me to hike this way, but it's a dead end.

– Can't you go down that way?

She moves closer to the edge. I grab her and say,

– Watch yourself. We don't want you falling. You could die.

– Like you care.

– Of course, I care.

– That's new.

She tries to move closer to the edge. I hold her back. She insists. My hands keep a hold of her. She says,
 - Did something die down there?
 - Probably. We're in the woods. Anything can happen. We should go.
 - Something definitely died down there. I can feel it.
 - We should go. It's getting late.
 - I'll bet I can tell you what kind of animal it is.
 - Please. Some things are better left unknown.
 - Says who?
 - We need to go.
 - Why are you acting weird?
 - I'm not acting weird. I don't want to leave you alone out here. That's all.
A gust of wind rises from the valley gusting with the force of an unruly ghost. It blows dirt into Tammy's eyes. I shelter mine. This gets Tammy to back away from the edge.

We end up at the coffee shop sitting at a table sipping our coffees, I ask,
 - Seriously, what were you doing out there? Do you even hike?
 - Today, apparently. But usually, no.
 - Why today?
 - I had an urge. It's a beautiful day, so why not?
Tammy sips her coffee and asks,
 - Why were you out there?
 - I had an urge. It's a beautiful day, so why not?
 - Touche'.
 - How's the medium business?

- There's something different about you. I can't pinpoint it.
- I'm the same. I did meet a girl.
- Maybe that's what it is. Good for you. What's her name?
- Monica.
- Monica what?
- Why do you care?
- There's the Eddie I'm used to.
- Her name is Monica Sellers.
- Black girl?
- You know her?
- Be careful. She's a little coo coo.
- Like you weren't. I got to go.

I storm out of there like the woman in the movie who just heard that her husband is cheating on her. In the movies, she doesn't look back. I don't either.

I spend the rest of the day meditating in my backyard. Maybe some answers to this mess will come to me. What comes to me is an urge to take a day off. I'm going to spend tomorrow at home to figure this mess out. Zero contact will be my motto for tomorrow.

# 27

## Day 27

My day of solitude starts with the sun shining its light on me and a feeling of goodness. I do some push-ups and sit-ups. Three sets of twenty-five to be exact. I don't need coffee due to the boost from the exercises. I wash my face and look in the bathroom mirror. I have a conversation with myself.

- You fucking killed someone. You had a chance
to tell the police and didn't. What the fuck is
wrong with you? It was self-defense. Was it?
Yes. It was. Why haven't bears eaten the body
yet? It's bullshit.
Before the rape, I had a thriving practice.
I went hiking regularly. My motorcycle brought
me joy. The only thing I was missing in life was
love. I was working on that.
Now, what do I have? Nothing. That's not
true. I have someone who wants to beat me up
and will want to kill me when he finds out that
I killed his best friend.
I have Monica. She is interested. Maybe too
interested in all of this, if you ask me. I like our

time together when we aren't dealing with the
"thing." Our sex is great. She gives me a fuzzy
feeling. We giggle. I feel blessed to have a girl
like her.

Would she still like me if none of this
happened? Could she put up with my boring
life? I don't fucking know, and I don't want to
think about it either. Right now, all I want to
do is enjoy our real-life moments.

Being alone is what got me into this mess.
If I weren't alone, then someone would have
been there to remind me that life is about love.
Someone could have stopped me from messing
with the motorcycle shop. Then I never would
have done anything. I'm supposed to say it's
better to regret things you do instead of things
you don't do. That's what I'm supposed to say.
Not sure it's true in this case.

I splash water on my face and stare into the eyes in the mirror.
What stares back at me are the eyes of a killer. I wish they were
the eyes of a life coach. I wish Golden Love could somehow save
me from this mess.

‐ There's one more thing that's bothering me. I
liked it. I liked the chase. I liked the fight. I
liked the kill. I especially liked how it felt
afterward. The energy flowing through me was
undeniable. I thought Nora filled my emptiness.
The kill was way better. For the first time since
being with Nora, I feel alive. I feel like a
superhero... I need a drink.

Alcohol is my best friend right now. We have many conversations. I've swallowed everything it says to me. It listens to every word slurred from my mouth. We have an understanding. We don't judge each other. It makes me not care. Together, we get me out of the house for a walk through the community.

While walking the suburban streets leading up to our small downtown, I find myself whistling "Amazing Grace." It makes me feel empowered like I know something no one else does.

A tree lining the sidewalk has a missing person poster hanging on it. I rip it down to get a closer look. It reads: "A Staple in our Community is Missing." There's a picture of David Undercuffler smiling and looking all wholesome.

- Fuck you. A fucking staple my ass. You
fucking deserved it.

A person is walking toward me from the other direction. I crinkle up the flyer and put it in my pocket. The person is a middle-aged woman carrying a bag of groceries. The woman glares at me as she passes. Either she saw me rip down the flyer or she knows that alcohol and I are hanging out today. I begin singing loudly,

- "Amazing grace how sweet the sound
Who saved a wretch like me.
I once was lost, but now am found,
was blind, but now I see."
The woman turns back to me and says,
- You're a wretch all right.
- What the fuck did I do? I'll tell you what I do.
I save this town from wretches. I was blind, but
now I see. The Amazing Grace is me!
She hurries away. I stumble onward with no destination.
- Community staple. Fuck You! If anyone

around here is a community staple, it's me. I'm the one who made things right. I'm the one who saved the day. Me. Not David Underfucker. Me. Me!

I peer through the fence of the motorcycle shop at the bikes. I wish my bike were running. It always gives me the feeling that I'm free to go or do anything. That is something I miss. Sure, day-drinking is something I can do, and I met a girl, but now I have to look over my shoulder. That's not freedom. For all I know, someone could be sneaking up on me right now. For no other reason other than I was in the wrong place at the wrong time. If only I wouldn't have been in the woods. I would never have seen anything. None of this would have happened. I say to myself,

 – Stay Golden. I got to Stay Golden.

One of the mechanics sees me pressed up against the fence. I salute him, so he knows that I'm good and appreciate motorcycles. He heads into the shop. A second or two later, he and the other workers are holding wrenches and walking towards me. I run.

My next stop is the bar. I'll fit right in with the other people drinking their lives away. We can talk about how we had different plans for our lives but something happened, and here we are. Something always happens is what I would say. It's getting back on the horse that keeps us alive. Right now, I don't even see a horse.

The bar door won't open. It seems to be stuck. No, it's just that I've been looking down the whole time and didn't see the sign. It reads: Bar closed until 5 p.m.

– Why today? Why!?

The obvious choice is to buy a bottle and binge the day away.
I sit on the curb with my face in my hands and cry.
 – Everything I know has changed...And me with
it. Look what I've become.
I dry my eyes with my palms. It doesn't seem to be working.
The sleeves of my shirt aren't working either. Good thing the
street is empty. I surely look like a total sap.
Fingers tap me on the shoulder. As my head rises from my
hands, the sun hurts my eyes. It's the Asian bar owner. She's
wearing one of those big summer hats that are woven together
and block the sun like Audrey Hepburn wore in "Breakfast at
Tiffany's." She also has a stylish red scarf around her neck. She
looks like a movie star. She asks,
 – Are you okay? Do you need something?
My puffy eyes gaze up at her. Her backlit silhouette makes her
look like an angel. I want to say something but am mesmerized
by her glow. She reaches out her hand and says,
 – Let me help you.
She pulls me up.
 – Thanks. It has been one of those days when
you have to make a decision but don't know
what to do.
 – Oh honey, always choose the better one.
 – The better one?
 – Always choose the sun, honey.
 – The sun?
 – The light.
 – Oh, the light. What happens when there is no
light?

– Come here and drink. I'm kidding, honey. Find it and follow it. That simple.
– Find it and follow it.
– That simple.
– Thanks. I have to go and find it.

New mission: Find my light.

Caffeine will help me with this task. Monica pops into my head while I drink my black coffee with no room. After all, this is our spot. The coffee shop is where we met. Our sex is great. She likes it hard and fast like I do. Could she be my light?

When was the last time I felt the power of the light? The first thing that comes to me is the drive home from the motorcycle shop after the kill, also when I was dumping the body. Come to think of it, everything having to do with the kill heightens my inner buzz.

I never had an urge to kill before. The thought never crossed my mind. Maybe at the motorcycle shop a few times but that's the kind of thing you don't act on.

There has to be something else. Eva. Going to jail and meeting the rapists there. The interrogation, which was scary at the time, lit me up too. Eva and my's crazy almost sex. That charged me up. Ever since giving up on life coaching, my life has lit up. More has happened lately than in the last few years of my life. I even have a potential girlfriend now.

If I were to life coach myself right now, I would say follow your bliss. It will save you and bring you happiness. It's a good idea except that my bliss is pointing toward craziness and killing.

Worry and coffee fill me. It's starting to feel like everyone is looking at me. Maybe the coffee shop patrons can sense something. What if they know? What if I said something out loud and didn't know it? I jump to my feet. The chair falls over. Some people look up from their computers. Oh my God, they know. I force the chair into the upright position and speed walk out of there. Speed walking doesn't cut it, so I run. My coffee burns my hand as I do. It slows me a second. I drink down some to prevent any more coffee abuse. It burns the top of my mouth. I spit it out and run home.

While running, one word pops into my head, Nora. My light shines the brightest with Nora. With her, I shine from love. She could be the one to save me. Out of the blue, I hear,

– Hey, Eddie. Why are you running?

It's Tammy. She is driving beside me in her same beat up Honda Accord that she has had for at least ten years now. I try my hardest not to let her lock onto my energy. I say,

– Can't a guy run?

– What were you really doing in the woods yesterday?

I slow down and cross to the other side of the street. Tammy follows with her car. She yells,

– You know I'll find out. I have ways.

I don't acknowledge her. I run between houses and disappear into the suburban landscape. I hear tires squeal to a stop. Then a guy yells,

– What the fuck is wrong with you? This is America. We drive on the right!

There's a knock at my door. I get up from my favorite chair. It's a director's chair with the words "Life Coach" printed on it. Suppose it's not as fitting as it once was. If I get a new one, what would it say? Killer. Nerves fill me as I'm about to open the door. Monica's smiling face greets me. She's wearing hip hugging jeans and a low cut T-shirt that show off her body quite nicely. The sight of her beautiful brown eyes calms me for a moment. I can't hide the worry. I say,

- Monica, we have a problem.
- Is it something this will help with?

She pulls a bottle of Patron Silver out of her bag. I say,

- It's big.
- What about this?

She plants her lips on mine. Her soft, luscious pillows give me a fuzzy feeling on the inside. I say,

- That could help. Let's try that again to be safe.

We hold each other and kiss. We kiss hard yet loving at the same time. A warmth fills me. Monica's eyes tell me that she feels the same. She says,

- I'm here now.
- Yeah, you are.
- What can be so terrible?
- Tammy, my ex who's a medium, knows or will know soon enough. She communicates with dead people.
- I know what a medium does, Eddie.
- What do we do?

The next thing I know, we're sitting in Monica's Infinity sedan. It's comfortable and warm. It has the full package with leather and all the fixings. The tequila bottle comes down from my lips. It fills me with its heat on this cold occasion. We've parked two houses down from Tammy's place. I can't help but take another shot of Tequila. Monica says,

- Slow down there, cowboy. We got a job to do.

– How can you be so calm?

– Eddie, this has to be done. That's how. You
know the plan.

I attempt to take another shot. Monica pulls the bottle from
my lips.

– Don't fuck this up.

– We have a history.

– Yeah, and since she has been the bane of your
existence. Stealing your energy and bothering
you at the coffee shop. You can't even walk
down the street.

– You're right.

– You got this. Text me the signal.

She kisses me on the lips and pushes me out the door. Slowly
my nervous legs walk me toward Tammy's place. I look back
at Monica. She waves me along. Fear stops me. Turning back
seems like a better idea. There has to be another way. If I walk
back to the car, I won't hear the end of it. And Monica is right.
Something needs to be done. But maybe not as planned. Maybe I
can work this out. Be strong. Be Golden. I take a breath and keep
walking. I march right up and knock like a man with purpose
would.

Tammy answers,

– Hey, Eddie. What are you doing here?

– Can we talk?

– What about?

– The woods.

– Come in.

Her house is nicer than I remember. It is full of adult things. It
has matching brown furniture in the living room. Metal shelves
and tables line the walls. It has a very rustic feel to it. I say,

- I like what you did with the place.
- I could clean a little. Let's talk in the kitchen.
Want a drink?
- Tequila straight.
- Somethings never change.
- Nope.

My eyes survey the area in search of clues to her intentions. My best guess would be that she wouldn't turn me in, but who knows. She likes to see me squirm. There are some papers around and some paintings of sunsets, but otherwise, her place gives no clues. On her refrigerator, a sign reads: Energy is Life. Life is Energy. Use it or be Used. Tammy hands me my drink. I say,

- "Energy is life. Life is energy. Use it or be used." I like that quote. Who said it?
- You don't know?
- I wouldn't be asking if I did.

Tammy raises her glass. I follow suit. She says,

- A Toast to the quote on the fridge and the life coach that said it. Here's to you, Eddie King.
- Did I say that? Cheers.

We both take sips. Not sure why I don't remember. I say,

- Well, I'm glad you like it. I have my moments.
- That was quite the run you did earlier.
- I was in the zone.
- Is that what you call it?
- Some things should be discussed in private.
- Do tell. That is why you're here.
- Let me ask you something. If you knew someone who did something not so good in the communities eyes, would you keep it a secret?

152

Now, it may not have been handled properly, but none-the-less it was for the better. Would you tell? Or rather, would you investigate using your medium powers even though you were asked not to?

- That's a tough one, Eddie.

- Even if the person assured you that it was for the greater good?

- Does this have to do with a person?

- Yes.

- What if there is a ghost and it finds me? They have a way of finding people they can relay messages through.

- Can you turn that off? Shut them out.

- It's not that easy. Being a medium is my business.

- Okay. Tammy, would you tell anyone? Like the police?

- I don't know. Why don't you tell me what happened first?

- Have you seen those signs for the missing kid around town?

- David Undercuffler?

My head nods in agreement. My shaky hand grabs the tequila. I slam the whole thing. I pull my phone out of my pocket and look at it then place it on the table in front of me. I say,

- May I have another?

Tammy slams her drink also. She always could drink. Tammy gives me a long look. She must be trying to feel me out. I wish she would just let me know if she would be cool with all of this. I type the text: "Can you walk the dog?" I don't send it. Stay

Golden echoes in my head. I smile at Tammy as she hands me the drink. She sits and says,

- So, what you're saying is you killed David Undercuffler and dumped his body in the woods. But you swear it was for the "greater good," as you call it. And you came over here to see if I was going to tell the police or try to investigate on my own. Is that the gist of it?

- You always could understand me like no other.

- How did it feel?

- It made me feel charged up.

- Would you do it again?

I sip my drink.

- I don't think so. But my energy-flow afterward felt stronger than an erupting volcano. That hasn't happened before. I got to tell you. It felt great.

- I want to feel like that.

- I want to feel like that all the time.

She has a glow in her eyes. I can't tell if it is good or bad. She says,

- Can you imagine the possibilities?

- One word comes to mind, superpower.

- Eddie, I'll make you a deal. If you can harness your energy while remembering the incident and let me touch you at that moment, then I will forget this whole conversation and the woods. Deal?

I sip my tequila again. Tammy's proposition sounds enticing but what will become of my energy? Could she take it all? Will I no longer be a battery of light for people? The bright side is no jail. I can put it all behind me and move on. I stick out my hand and say,

   – Deal.

   – Good choice. When can we do this, Eddie?

   – Tomorrow or the next day.

   – I have memory problems and don't want anything to slip out by mistake.

   – Fine. Tomorrow is good. Can I use your bathroom?

   – It's through there.

Cold water splashes my face and gives me some relief. I may not like Tammy and don't necessarily like our agreement, but she doesn't deserve to die over this. Tammy's proposition is the best outcome. We can go on with our lives.

   – Excellent work, no more killing. Thank you, God.

I pat dry my face then head back to the kitchen to say goodbye before Monica gets worried.

When I get to the kitchen, Tammy isn't there. I look toward the front door. As I do, Tammy's body drops to the floor. Monica is standing over her with a bloody knife. Tammy reaches up. Monica is stabbing over and over. I scream,

   – NO!!!

Tammy's eyes blank just as I get there. Her body stills with lifelessness. Monica, on the other hand, her eyes are filled with life. She looks like an animal who just won her kingdom. She looks at me like I could be next. I say,

   – I didn't send you the signal. We didn't have to.

   – That was fucking wild. I feel fucking great!

Monica presses her lips against mine so hard that I forget that they're pillows of lusciousness. I break from it.

- Fuck. She didn't need to die.
- Fuck that bitch!
- She said she wasn't going to tell.
- Quit your whining and help me roll her up.
Monica pulls a Mexican blanket out of her backpack.
- You brought a blanket?
- I was a girl scout. Help me roll.

We put the body in the same trash can in my garage then go in the house. Monica jumps my bones as soon as we step foot inside. We immediately begin tongue wrestling and fondling each other's body. It probably looks like one of those comedic makeout scenes where they extremely overdo it. I assure you, she isn't acting.

We quickly find ourselves on the bed naked. Monica is different this time. She's fully connected. It's something I have never experienced before. She's all-in. I want to be all-in but considering how the night went, I can't. Monica is giving me the best ride of my life, and it's still hard to get into it. Monica stops,

- Is everything okay?
- Yeah. It's just that you seem so into it and connected. You've never been this way before. It's throwing me off my game.
- Oh, Eddie baby, you're the best. But you think too much. Now shut up and fuck me!

The sex is incredible. I'm still not all-in, but Monica makes up for that. After we both cum and are laying there, everything feels better. Everything seems like it will be alright. This feeling has alluded me for quite some time. Monica rolls over and kisses me. She nibbles on my lips and whispers,

– This may seem weird considering the night
we had, but I have to go.

A sense of relief fills me. I could use some time to figure this
all out. I say,

– That's okay. I could use some sleep. We have
to "you know," tomorrow.

– I'm off at 2 p.m. Love you.

Monica exits. I fall back on the bed.

– Did she just say I love you?

# 28

# Day 28

- Eddie, Oh Eddie. Eddie!

It was a horrible night. It seemed like every ten minutes I kept waking up to someone saying my name. I sit up in fear the first few times. After the tenth time or so, I only open my eyes and look around. No one is ever there. But I swear that I hear my name. Rest is not something that happened to me last night. Hopefully, some coffee can help me shake this grogginess.

I sip my coffee while watching the news. The same story is on. "What happened to David Undercuffler?" The cute news reporter who interviewed me about the motorcycle shop interviews people around town. She looks better on TV. In person, her makeup is a bit overwhelming. The people she interviews say, "I didn't know him, but I heard he was a good guy." "I sure hope they find him." "Who knows, maybe he left this town for a fresh start, that's what I want to do." "What is this city coming to? Soon you won't be able to walk down the street." The news reporter ends the segment with "Our hearts go out to David's family. If anyone knows his whereabouts, please come forward. Your family misses you, David, please come home. We all miss you David Undercuffler." Here's what I say to that,

- Fuck David Undercuffler. He's a fucking rapist.
There ain't a damn thing wrong with this town
except for the news. A total bunch of idiots.
A text comes from Monica. It says,
: I'm feeling sweet like honey. Let's meet in the
woods at 3 p.m.
Even though I just drank coffee, I feel a nap is in order. My
burning eyes become heavy while watching the Price Is Right.
Flashes of Tammy's body falling to the ground fill my head. Her
image is like a broken record.

She didn't need to die. She would have kept her word. She
always did. Everything would have been fine if Monica didn't
jump the gun.

Another attempt to close my eyes is in order. Again, Tammy is
there. It's like she's haunting me. My nap turns out to be exactly
like my night of sleep, unsuccessful. I attempt my connection
exercises. Breathing deep relaxes me a bit. When I close my
eyes to connect, Tammy's face is there. She's saying, "This is
your fault!" My eyes open abruptly.

- I'm fucked.

My eyes close again. Tammy is floating in front of me. She
looks pissed. When she was like this when we were going out, I
would leave because she wouldn't hear anything except herself.
I say,

- I didn't want this to happen.
- You killed me, you asshole. I am going to
make your life a living hell.
- Tammy, please. I didn't kill you.
- Tell me you didn't put that bitch, you call a
friend, up to killing me.
- Her name is Monica. And that is not what

happened.

- Your life is fucked, buddy.

Tammy disappears. As she does, I say,

- Please, let me explain.

I open my eyes. I look at the clock and only five minutes passes.

- Fuck. I just want to sleep. If there is a God, please help me to sleep. Even just for ten minutes. Please, God!

My phone rings. I want to throw it across the room. It's my mom. We have the deal of always answering the phone. Today seems like a good day for an exception. She calls back again. I scream,

- Fuck!!!!!!

I answer the phone.

- Hey, Mom. How's it going?
- I'm just coming back from the golf club. Our team came in second.
- Did you win something?
- Honey, just playing is winning. And we won a gift certificate to the country club which we blew on drinks. How are you?
- Honestly, I couldn't sleep last night and feel horrible.
- How's your blood pressure?
- I don't think that's the cause.
- Do you think that it's because you gave up coaching? No one likes an aimless person.
- Who said I gave up coaching?
- You did.
- I don't remember telling you that.

‒ You must have. Or maybe I just knew. That
sometimes happens when you have kids.
‒ I wouldn't say I gave it up. It's more like I'm on
hiatus. No one wants a failed life coach.
‒ Enough of that talk. No one is perfect. Not
even Jesus. Get back up on that horse.
‒ When I'm coaching, all I feel is validation for
my work and worry. What about love, joy,
happiness, even hate? I'm human.
‒ Sorry, what was that?
‒ I need to feel too. What about me?
‒ It's loud here. I have to go.
‒ Enjoy yourself.

I hang up and fall back on the couch. Maybe drinking is in
order.


Getting Tammy's body to the woods is a lot harder than the
first body. Maybe it's the four tequila shots. The lack of sleep
isn't helping either. Five times I have to drop her to rest. Serves
her right. She deserves a beating. Hopefully, she didn't hear
me say that. As I hoist her on my shoulder for the home stretch,
I see Monica at the drop spot. My first smile of the day fills my
face. It feels like I'm exiting a cave and seeing the sun for the
first time. Her silhouette is the lighthouse to guide me out. A
fuzzy feeling fills me at the thought of our lips touching. I trip. I
try to land on Tammy for a cushion. It doesn't work. What does
work is the rock that smacks me straight in the lip. It feels like
I've been punched in the mouth. Again, I leave blood in these
woods. I kick Tammy for revenge. It helps me forget about the
pain.

Monica greets me with a kiss when I get to the edge. I fall into her arms like a traveler crossing the desert who reaches his lost love. I don't want to move. All that I want to do is stay in her arms forever. She notices my lack and says,

– Is everything okay?

– Now that you're here, it is.

– You look like shit.

– I didn't sleep at all last night.

– Why not?

– Bad dreams.

– What about?

– I don't want to talk about it. Can we just do this so I can cuddle with you in bed?

– Cuddling sounds nice.

– Doesn't it? Give me a minute to put on my game face.

In the exact spot where the rapist once was is now where Tammy's body lays. Her body is shades of blue and purple. Her odor is on the rise. I say,

– Before we honey her, I'd like to comment.

Tammy, you taught me a lot about what I wanted. Thank you. At times you have violated my space, and that makes me upset. For the record, I didn't want this, Monica did.

– Is this really necessary?

– We did have a relationship.

– Seriously?

Monica squeezes honey all over Tammy's head. My hands join in. Monica says,

– We could call ourselves the Honey Gang.

– Is two people a gang?

– What about the Honey Killers?

- That sounds like we killed our loved ones or used honey to do it.
- Well, what do you got, smart guy?
- If we had to be called something, what about The Honey Droppers?
- Hmmm. The Honey Droppers. It has a nice ring to it. What about Honey Mummy and the Droppers.
- What are we a band?
- Do you play, Eddie?
- I own a guitar but don't play it much. Do you play?
- I'm Honey Mummy, the singer. You're the beat dropper.
- So I'm the DJ, and you're the rapper?
- I'm Honey Mummy, and my hands hurt.
Let's roll this body, and cover her in dirt.
Over the edge, she will fly.
Wave your hands, and say bye-bye.
- Not bad. But your flow needs some work. We could be on to something.
We roll the body and watch her body smash on the rocks and trees all the way down. I say,
- Good riddance, Tammy. Rest in peace.
- You hungry?
- I thought we were going to cuddle.
- After. Food will do you good.


We get a nice Italian dinner at Vitiello's Place. It's the best Italian restaurant in town. They have the checked tablecloths and a three piece band singing Italian classics. I don't know

Italian, but the music is fun. They bring you a pizza slice as an appetizer. It's always delicious. Sometimes, the pizza is what to order, other times, like tonight, lasagna is the best. Monica gets the chicken parmesan. It too is delightful. Monica's foot begins massaging my inner thighs. Her toes are wiggling just the right way. Although the food is delicious, it's hard to focus. Monica is looking at me with an "I want to eat you look." My eyes survey the dining room. No one is paying attention. I smile and say,

- Hey Honey Mummy, do you come here often?
- What kind of question is that?
- Hey, Honey Mummy, how's the sausage?

Monica growls at me and says,

- Well done and Hard.
- Is that how you like the Dropper, well done and Hard?

Her toes clench my hard cock. It makes me practically jump out of my seat. Our waitress comes by to see if everything is alright. While squirming, I say,

- Everything is great. Can you box these up for us? We really must be going.

The sex tonight may be the best sex of my life. Monica, now known to me as Honey Mummy, seems so genuine and so perfectly in touch with me. I, the Dropper, am so perfectly in tune with her too. Our connection may have just moved into the real-life undeniable category.

# 29

## Day 29

I wake up on high alert hearing Tammy call my name. Monica is sound asleep. She is faintly snoring. It's the cutest thing. Why does she get to sleep and not me? Why doesn't Tammy bother her? This is bullshit. Please stop, Tammy. Please, stay away from both of us. No one deserves this.

Tammy leaves me alone long enough to fall asleep. As soon as I begin dreaming, Tammy is sitting in a chair at the coffee shop sipping a drink. She looks the way she did when we went out. Long red hair, tight jeans, and a yellow shirt that says "Sunshine." It's the shirt I got her on Valentine's Day before we went camping in Arizona. I always wanted her to wear that shirt and she never would. The coffee shop is empty except for her. There are two drinks in front of her on the table. One must be mine. I sit and sip the coffee. Tammy says,

   – I'm going to be quick. We don't want you
   sleeping long. The only way to get me to leave
   you alone is for you to get rid of Monica.
   – What? No. We're starting something that is
   undeniable. I will not.
   – Then never sleep again. Insomnia is an ugly

thing.

– I'll break-up with her.

– That's not what I mean. I mean drop the Honey
Mummy with the others.

– Kill Monica? I don't think so.

My eyes open. I feel like a cat on a watch. My eyes dart around the room in search of safety. Of course, Monica is sleeping. I give her a kiss on the forehead then find something to occupy my time.

Monica enters the living room where I'm attempting to watch TV. It's not catching my interest, but Monica sure is. She looks like an angel from heaven. She's wearing pink panties, and that's it. Her perfect body is on display, and it looks glorious. At this moment, everything means nothing and only she exists. A smile fills my face. It's not a "tell-all" smile. It's more of a "this feels excellent" smile. She stomps over dragging her feet like she's a little kid and kisses me. Her smell is divine. Her bed head is blessed. Her lips, don't even get me started.

– Monica, I think we're having a real-life
moment. One of those that you remember
forever. Do you feel it?

Monica pours two glasses of water. She hands me one and sits on my lap. Our lips meet once again. As her body presses against mine, I forget my insomnia and go straight to Cloud 9. Goosebumps roll across my body. We both sip our waters while staring into each other's eyes. Monica says,

– With you, I feel everything.

There's no better way to start your day than morning sex. Should I call it morning sex or morning making love? Either way, I love it. It seems like Monica does too. It's a damn shame that mornings can't last forever.

Reality sets in as soon as Monica leaves. Everything sucks. Monica not being here so she can comfort me is the suckiest of all.

I have to pee, and the toilet seat is down. I don't have the energy to put it up. As I pee all over the it, I yell,
   – I'm a guy. You're supposed to be up. Mother
   fucker. Fuck you toilet!
I kick the toilet and hurt my foot. I limp to the kitchen and sit by the window. I try meditating. My attempts fail due to burning eyes, body pain, and a racing brain of unclarity. Stillness alludes me, and so do answers of how to stop this.

Food is next on my list. I go back to basics and have a PBJ. At least I attempt to have a PBJ. I can't get the lid off of the Goddamn jelly. I want to smash it on the ground. And almost do. I run hot water on the top. I bang it on the table's edge. Nothing works. I squeeze the jar in my hand in an attempt to induce pain on it.
   – You suck, jelly!
I toss the pain-in-my-ass, good-for-nothing, jelly jar in the trash. A peanut butter sandwich will have to do. While I'm spreading the peanut butter, of course, the bread rips.
   – Mother Fucker! You piece of shit, cock
   sucking, sandwich!
I throw the knife into the sink and storm off for some fresh air. I return in about a minute or so. It could be ten. Nothing is sure anymore. I grab the sandwich and shove it in my mouth.

Chewing is hard with the large amount of peanut butter on it. It's hard to swallow. I spit it out when my jaw starts hurting. A smaller bite may work better. I don't remember PB sandwiches tasting this bland. I wish I could have opened the jelly jar.

I wash out the body mover a.k.a. trash can. It still has a faint smell of death lingering. It's nothing a full blast hose can't fix. Water splashes back on me. I throw down the hose and storm off.

   – Mother Fucking Hose! You piece of shit!

When I return, the yard is one giant puddle. My feet become soaking wet.

   – This is all your fault, Tammy. Fuck You!

When the smell is gone, I show my dominance and throw the trash can hoping it will land upside down. It doesn't. I slam the trash can upside down and slap it to stay. Filled with the rage of wet feet and insomnia, I grab the hose and shoot it right on the top of my head.

   – Wash it away. Wash it all away!

My phone rings. It's Monica.

   – What?

   – Why are you yelling, baby?

   – The lack of sleep is killing me.

   – Listen to my voice. Listen how it makes you calm and fills you with love. Do you feel it?

   – I do.

   – I do too. Eddie, could this be a real-life moment? Aren't we so good together? Nothing but us. Nothing but love.

   – Monica, I... You're the best.

- I'll be over right after work. Can you find a way to fill your time?
- Besides thinking of you? I don't know.
- I'll see you soon, baby.

A proper shower is in order. I want to keep the feeling going that Monica gave me. I like how when your head is under the shower, and you can't hear anything but the running water. It's like nothing else exists. It gets me thinking. Can people get caught up in the kill and not be killers? Yeah, I killed someone. I don't want to do it again. The energy flow that comes afterward would be nice to have again. The killing part wasn't so fun. The second time, it was sad seeing Tammy lying on the floor lifeless.

Monica seems to be glowing more than ever. Just thinking of her gives me a warm feeling. Although, she does look way too into the kill. After the murder of Tammy, she shined the brightest. I didn't say anything because I was in shock. Today, she's been glowing all day. Her light helps me keep going. It's time for me to feed off of someone else's energy for once. We could be good together. She could be the jelly to my peanut butter.

I sit on the floor of the hallway that connects my kitchen to the bedroom. My eyes close. Sleep is the very thing I need, but I'm scared to attempt. I rub my eyes open. The last person I want to see right now is Tammy. She was bad enough alive but dead she is far worse.

Ten minutes of sleep and everything would be better. I'll be able to think straight. I'll be able to act like a human being again.

Suddenly, I'm sitting in an art studio. Tammy is sitting behind an easel painting. She has the paintbrush in her mouth. She's using her fingers to paint. She pulls the brush from her mouth and says,

– What's taking so long? Before you answer that,
I painted you something.

She shows me the painting. It's me sleeping with a smile on my face and a caption that reads: Zzzzzzzz.

– Do you like it?
– I love it.
– That can be you again. All you have to do is
kill Monica.
– I won't.
– Suit yourself.

Tammy rips the canvas into pieces. She smiles while doing so. I open my eyes. I'm still in the hallway. I need to keep moving.


The sun feels ten times brighter than it has ever been in my life. It's so bright that I can barely open my eyes. The sun is usually a Godsend, but today it hurts my whole body. I wish it would hide for a while. It's making this mile walk seem next to impossible. A senior woman passes me on the sidewalk. She smiles and says,

– Everything okay, young man?
With what little smile I can muster, I say,
– Enjoying a stroll.
She smirks like an old person would and says,
– It's the secret to life, you know.

She seems like a race car. My speed is more like a weighed down VW bus going up a mountain. The bright side to all of this is that I have time to kill. The not so bright side is everything else.

My eyes become heavier than Tammy's dead body. I take

shelter under a tree to rub them open. I must have dozed off while standing because almost immediately, I see Tammy. She's sitting in the branches of the tree above. She looks down on me while licking a giant lollipop and says,

  – Hey, Eddie. You didn't think you could get
  away from me that easily did you?
  – Please leave me alone. I didn't kill you,
  Monica did.
  – So sad. Hey, guess what? I'm learning how to
  communicate with you when you're awake.
  Isn't that great? We can be together all of the
  time.

My eyes open as my body slides off the tree. The ground catches me nicely. The tree's root jabs me in the side and knocks the wind out of me. Or, Tammy found a way to punch me in the stomach. I'm hoping it was the tree's root. I roll on the ground wheezing for air. This makes me feel more awake. I attempt speed walking to the coffee shop before this feeling wears off. It seems like I'm running. My speed walk is fast. At least it feels that way until a lady passes me with a baby stroller while talking on the phone.

The outside sitting area at the coffee shop is empty. It's just like my dream. This stops me dead in my tracks. Fear runs through me as I look around. Tammy is nowhere in sight. I close my eyes and step on my foot. It hurts. My eyes open abruptly. I must not be dreaming. It's weird that the coffee shop is so dead empty. It makes me wonder what everyone knows that I don't. What is the universe trying to tell me? I'm not dead.

The barista gives me her usual smirk. I ask,

– Why is it so dead in here? Is there something I need to know?

– We get these dead spots periodically. Think of it as a blessing. You don't have to wait in line.

– Cheers to dead spots. I mean, to no more dead spots.

I raise my coffee and wink at her. She smiles her barista smirk. I sip my coffee and say,

– Fuck that's hot.

She smiles her barista smirk again and says,

– Have an alive day.

I look at her with my burning red eyes. Her smile is that of a nice person. It's alive and full. It's as if she cracked herself up. A chuckle fills me too. I raise my coffee into the air in salute,

– To an alive day.

It feels eerie sitting at a coffee shop all alone. It's as if I'm waiting for something. I hope that doesn't mean that something is waiting for me. This gives me an idea. Ideas are hard to come by when you lack sleep. I text Monica to meet me here instead. She texts me back a smiley face. A sense of accomplishment fills me. Who needs sleep when you can have good ideas like that?

Who am I kidding? The killing needs to stop. So does this lack of sleep. Just because I can have one of these brilliant ideas doesn't mean I can think straight. I begin breathing exercises in hopes to connect. My hands don't tingle like they usually do. My inner chanting gets sidetracked after every line by thoughts of how pointless this is. Tammy's voice catches my ear. It says,

– Can't connect, huh? Such a pity.

My eyes open. I rub them profusely. Burning hot coffee fills me in hopes to keep me awake.

I let the water run in the bathroom until it's colder than winter in Chicago then splash it over my whole head. My body stiffens. A few more splashes and my head begins to hurt. It's a good hurt. I look at myself in the mirror. Goddamn, do I look terrible. I hadn't looked this bad since New Year's Eve 2000 when I accidentally drank a Gatorade spiked with enough speed for three people. I put on my sunglasses and go back to waiting for Monica.

A guy is ordering a coffee. I say,
– Finally, this place isn't a dead spot.
The guy turns with his coffee. It's Patrick Doyle. He sees me. I smirk for the second time all day. It's not a playful smirk either. My eyes center with purpose. It must be clear to him what is about to happen because he throws his coffee at me. The burning hot coffee hits me square in the chest. My reflexes aren't particularly fast right now. Patrick flips a table to block me and runs. I pull myself up. I look at the barista and say,
– I guess it's not dead anymore.
I take a big sip of coffee, then chase him.
We run through the streets of our small town. Shortness of breath fills me. Patrick is getting away. I have to run faster. I breathe slower and attempt to connect while running. It works. I feel my hands tingle. Energy flows throughout my body. I channel it into my legs and focus on catching Patrick. The gap between us shortens. He's only about twenty feet in front of me.

He runs around the corner and down an alley. The alley is small and only one-way. Empty trash cans flank its sides. Otherwise, it's empty. This is where I catch this fucker. I'm not sure what I'm going to do when that happens. I am confident that it is good to be chasing him for once. A car drives down the alley from the other side. It completely blocks him in. He has nowhere to run. He stops and turns toward me. I say,

– It's not fun, is it?

– Please don't kill me.

– Kill you? No. I want you to suffer like Mary Levitt suffered.

Patrick turns back toward the car. The car revs its engine. Monica pops her smiling head out the window and waves. I say,

– I too have a partner.

Patrick turns back toward me.

– It was Dave's idea. I swear. I didn't want to do it. He made me.

– That's not what I witnessed.

– You were there?

– That's right. I saw most of it.

– You're to blame too, then. You're just as bad as we are.

– Me? I'm doing nothing but righting a wrong. You're the wrong.

Monica peels out. Her car slams into Patrick. He flies into the trash cans. I check on him. His head is bleeding. Blood is coming from his mouth. His body is lifeless and limp. Monica runs up. She stands beside me and looks down at him. She says,

– Wow! That was brilliant.

My silent eyes look at her. She hugs me and begins kissing me intensely. Her body gyrates against mine. Mine joins in until I'm hard as a rock. As much as I think sex is a good idea, we have to separate. I break from our embrace.

– We have to go. Let's put him in the trunk.

We drag him to the car. His body slides through the spilled

one is shining from me as well. We look at each other smiling. After a few moments, Monica points to the back seat. I ask,

   – You want to have sex?

   – I do, but. The blanket.

I grab the Mexican blanket that's on the floor. Under the blanket is a gallon of honey. I look at her. She says,

   – I was a Girl Scout.

We wrap the body and together carry it into the woods. I have the top half, and she has the bottom. It's a lot easier with two people. Monica wants to break where the rape happened. We drop the body, and she pulls me in for a kiss. She says,

   – Fuck me.

   – Here?

She pulls the blanket down from Patrick's head. She opens his eyes and props his head against a rock. She begins unbuckling her belt and says,

   – Right here. Right now.

She takes off her pants and begins sucking my cock. When I become hard, which doesn't take long, she bends over a rock.

   – Fuck me, Eddie. Fuck me like you love me.

There is something exhilarating about having sex after you share a love ceremony with someone. Also, having sex to show the dead rapist what sex is supposed to look like, or should I say what lovemaking is supposed to look like, is such a thrill. It's the lovemaking of all lovemaking.

The sun is going down as we get to the drop spot. It's a pretty orange sunset. We pause to look at it. I begin yawning. Monica rubs my shoulders and says,

   – We're almost there, baby.

– I have to keep moving.

I use what little energy I can muster and begin covering the body with honey. Monica looks over the edge. She says,

– The bodies are still there.

I join her at the edge.

– Bears should have eaten them by now.

– They didn't.

– Help me roll him over.

Monica squeezes honey over Patrick's backside while I look over the edge. Why haven't bears eaten them yet? Bears love honey. Weird. Hopefully, they're decomposing. Monica says,

– Help me.

We roll his body over the edge. We stand and watch him hit the rocks and trees as he plummets to the bottom. I move behind Monica and rub her shoulders. She moans in delight. It feels good to have someone. I smile. We take in this real-life moment.

Tammy's voice inside my head breaks me from my tranquility. It says:

– "Do it. This is your chance, Eddie. Push her.
Then you can rest. I can rest. All of this will
be over. Do it! Do it now, Eddie! It's for the
greater good. DO IT!


The drive home is a quiet one. My first stop is an alley behind two empty houses. At least, they look empty. If they aren't, they sure are neglected. I park her car and give the doors and the dash a rub down.

It's about a half-mile to my place. The walk will do me good. I'm so incredibly tired but have an overwhelming sense of closure. I'm not sure what will happen or what it all means.

I am certain that it's over. Honestly, I don't know about that either.

Making it home is my sole goal. Walking might not be the right word for what I'm doing. Zombie-ing home might be a better description. A few blocks from the car is a street grate. That is where I drop the keys. The only thing left to do is make it home and sleep.

The first thing I do is a shot of bourbon. Just as I'm about to take another shot, the doorbell rings. I'm far too tired to be concerned. I slam the shot and answer the door. It's hard to see even with the outside light on.

Standing in the doorway is Nora. She is as radiant as ever. She's wearing a pink lace-lined top with dark colored skinny jeans and boots. She looks wholesome and badass at the same time. A half-smile covers my face. It should be more but considering. She says,

- Hi, Eddie.
- What are you doing here?
- Can I come in?
- It's kind of a bad time. Can you come back tomorrow?
- Is everything okay? You look like shit.
- It has been a hell of a ride. I'll see you tomorrow. Okay?
- Morning work? I'll bring some coffee.
- Not too early.
- Take care of yourself, Eddie.

I try my hardest to muster up a smile and say,

- You're the best, Nora.

I close the door and make my way to my bed. Everything

seems so surreal. It's hard to get undressed, so I don't finish. My head hits the pillow, and I'm out.

# 30

# Day 30

My buzzing phone wakes me. I ignore it the first few times and go back to sleep. The doorbell begins ringing repeatedly. The pillow covering my head doesn't block out the noise, so I reluctantly get up. Still half-dressed, I stumble to the door. My eyes burn from a good night's sleep cut short. The sun shining through the windows doesn't help much either. I open the door without thinking. The sun blasts me right in the face which almost knocks me over. With maximum effort and a handmade visor, I'm able to make out who it is. It's Nora in all of her glory. She's wearing a cute yellow sundress, large sunglasses, and knee-high black boots. There is a package beside her. She has coffee in each hand. I pinch myself, it hurts, so I smile. She says,

- Rise and shine sleepy head. I got coffee.
- What time is it?
- 1130 a.m.
- Come in. You look great.
- Thanks. The coffee is a little cold. I've been here since 10 a.m.
- What's the package?

– I don't know. It was here.

I take a few gulps of the coffee. My head pops up a bit from its strength. I grab the package. The label says it's from Cycle World in California. Nora watches my interest. She says,

– I got you a black eye.

– How many shots is that?

– It's two espresso shots mixed with coffee.

I attempt to open the package but can't. I say,

– That's some good coffee.

Nora helps me open the box. The tape is too much for me to handle. My eyes get bigger than the sun when I see what's in there. It's my exact motorcycle tank. And it's in perfect condition. I look at Nora and say,

– This is fucking great. You're the best!

Nora looks in the box. On the packing slip is a note. Nora reads it to me,

– It says: "Thought you might like this.

Love Monica." Who's Monica?

Nora's demeanor changes to defensive and let-down at the same time. I say,

– A girl I used to know. Wow, this is fucking
great. I'm going to imagine that you got this for
me.

– That's not right.

– It's better this way. Trust me.

I give Nora a hug. She doesn't hug me back. I say,

– So, what's the occasion?

– It's good to see you too Eddie, jeez.

– I'm sorry to sound crass. I haven't slept
much lately.

– Let's sit.

We sit at my little kitchen table which is so full of clutter that our coffees barely fit. Nora's soft hands grab mine. A warm sensation floods through me like a peaceful stream flowing through a bed of flowers. She squeezes my hands and says,

– I've been thinking what to say for weeks now.

I figured short and sweet is the best way.

– Should I be worried?

Her hands squeeze mine even tighter. Her beautiful blue eyes fix on me. I have to look down. They're too much to take in. I smile as her loving energy fills me. Our eyes meet again. She exhales like a little kid would before a speech. Then says,

– Here goes, ever since our connection, my life
has turned upside down. Everything that was
normal and right became strange and almost
cold. It's the weirdest thing. I'm not sure that I
like it. I don't know how to deal with it. So, I
came back to see.

– See what?

– ...If the same thing is happening to you.

I look her straight in her beautiful eyes and say,

– It has been the strangest month of my life.

She smirks then she coyly looks down. She squeezes my hands. It feels very welcoming. She looks up with the most beautiful look I have ever seen. I'm talking more beautiful than the heavens. How Nora radiates right now must be what Nelson Mandela meant about shining your light. Her light warms my whole body. It probably sizzles the entire block. She says,

– Do you think it's the world telling us
something?

I jump up, knock my chair to the floor, and pull her close. We hold each other and kiss. Our kiss is one for the record books. I don't think anyone has ever had a kiss this spectacular and this right. The energy inside me doesn't light me up like a Christmas tree. It lights me up like Times Square on New Year's Eve. Probably even brighter. Nothing in my life has ever felt like this. It's pure undeniable bliss. She breaks from the kiss. I look her over. She says,

- Is this one of those real-life moments you always talk about?
- Better.

I pull her in, and we kiss. I don't ever want this to stop. We break just long enough to say,

- I love you, Nora.
- I love you, Eddie.

I open my eyes, and I'm lying on the cold, damp ground of the woods. I'm not sure how I got here or what happened. I touch the back of my head, and there is a bump with some clumpy half-dried blood in my hair. It's almost dark and very hard to see. I say,

- Hello? Anyone here?

My cellphone light shines around for a sign of what happened. Nothing seems to be out of the ordinary. I wander out of the woods. When I get to my car, everything seems normal except for me. I look at myself in the mirror.

- Fuck. Was any of that real?

THE END

# Notes

Thanks for reading. If you would like to comment on this book, please send an email to:

DiaryofaFailedLifeCoach@Gmail.com